When eccentric Uncle Patrick gave Freddie an ancient map of the world for his birthday, it seemed an odd gift for a 13-year-old, but Freddie was thrilled by the unusual present from his favourite relative. Little did he know that the mysterious map was about to turn his world upside down!

Mounted on his bedroom wall, the antique map bristled with untold secrets, ones it seemed it was willing to share with Freddie, as it sucked him into a wildly spinning vortex, and past myriad portals into other lands and times.

One minute Freddie was in his perfectly normal bedroom, and the next – well, he found himself in Nepal in 1989, years before he had even been born.

With no way of knowing how or *if* he would ever get home again, Freddie began to explore, only to realise that the vortex had not taken him there by chance – he had a mission to fulfil! Encountering adversaries at every turn, including a mysterious enemy known only as the Collector, it seemed that the chances of him fulfilling the task were slim at best.

But Freddie Malone doesn't give up so easily...

A FREDDIE MALONE ADVENTURE

A JEWEL IN THE SANDS OF TIME

CLIVE MANTLE

AWARD PUBLICATIONS LIMITED

To find out more about the adventures
of Freddie Malone, please visit:

www.freddiemalone.com
www.clivemantle.com
🅕 *@theadventuresoffreddiemalone*

ISBN 978-1-78270-363-1

Cover design by Patrick Knowles
Photographs: Dimos/Shutterstock.com (cover),
Morozov67/Shutterstock.com (p267), agsaz/Shutterstock.com (p270)
Map and text illustration by Angie Hewitt

First published by Award Publications Limited 2019

Published by Award Publications Limited,
The Old Riding School, Welbeck,
Worksop, S80 3LR

www.awardpublications.co.uk

19 1

Printed in the United Kingdom

For Carla and Harry

If–

If you can keep your head when all about you
    Are losing theirs and blaming it on you,
If you can trust yourself when all men doubt you,
    But make allowance for their doubting too;
If you can wait and not be tired by waiting,
    Or being lied about, don't deal in lies,
Or being hated, don't give way to hating,
    And yet don't look too good, nor talk too wise:

If you can dream – and not make dreams your master;
    If you can think – and not make thoughts your aim;
If you can meet with Triumph and Disaster
    And treat those two imposters just the same;
If you can bear to hear the truth you've spoken
    Twisted by knaves to make a trap for fools,
Or watch the things you gave your life to, broken,
    And stoop and build 'em up with worn-out tools:

If you can make one heap of all your winnings
  And risk it on one turn of pitch-and-toss,
And lose, and start again at your beginnings
  And never breathe a word about your loss;
If you can force your heart and nerve and sinew
  To serve your turn long after they are gone,
And so hold on when there is nothing in you
  Except the will which says to them: "Hold on!"

If you can talk with crowds and keep your virtue,
  Or walk with Kings – nor lose the common touch,
If neither foes nor loving friends can hurt you,
  If all men count with you, but none too much;
If you can fill the unforgiving minute
  With sixty seconds' worth of distance run,
Yours is the Earth and everything that's in it,
  And—which is more—you'll be a Man, my son!

Rudyard Kipling, 1895

A Jewel
in the Sands
of Time

Prologue

In a cold, dark basement, a long way from where you are reading these words, the Collector sat at his writing desk inspecting a huge yellow gemstone under a solitary light. The elderly man scrawled on a piece of folded white card, using a quill dipped in vivid turquoise ink.

And many years ago, in a silent and ancient tomb, also a long way from you, there lay a king in his dark resting place. A long-dead boy king who was always at the mercy of those who would seek to possess his fabulous wealth. Close by the king, a small carved scarab beetle guarded the pharaoh through the twelve stages of night on his journey to the next life.

The Collector wanted to turn back time, steal the priceless artefact for himself and deny the joy of its discovery to the rest of the world. He also craved a precious liquid, a legendary elixir which if taken would prolong his life – the seconds, minutes and hours of which were trickling through his twisted fingers like fine desert sand as he neared his worldly end. He calculated that the two treasures could easily be collected together, or so he hoped.

Around him in the cavernous basement were dozens of cabinets containing many of the world's missing wonders, which he had acquired by one foul means or another. He moved towards the farthest display, running his fingers over the glass of several others as he passed. Even now, after all these years, there was still room for a treasure that was yet to be stolen. He unlocked the door of the last cabinet and with a shaky hand smoothed the velvet interior.

On it he placed the huge, yellow Florentine Diamond, tinkering with its position until he was satisfied that it caught the available light. Almost immediately his eyes moved from the priceless gemstone to the empty expanse to its right. He lovingly stroked the velvet cloth and whispered, "Of course, be patient. Not long now. You will soon have a treasure."

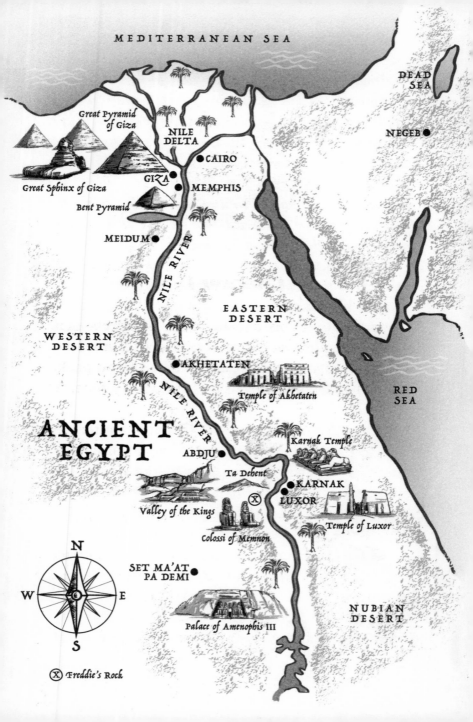

Chapter 1

Connor weighed up two handfuls of sweets that were being auditioned for the trip of a lifetime: the rectangular chews, which would be easier to pack, versus the chocolate raisins and strawberry rope. A tough call.

He uttered a weary sigh. Connor wanted to make room for them all, but he had to discipline himself. Today was supposed to be the start of his new healthy regime. He had to get fit if he wanted to accompany Freddie on his next adventure.

Mr Kapoor coughed politely.

"Would you mind standing to one side please, Connor, whilst I attend to my other valued customers?"

He quickly served the queue, but by now Connor was musing over a completely new set of sugary possibilities.

Ten minutes later and back with his original choice of sweets, he wandered along the high street towards Freddie's house. Connor was as happy as he could remember, despite his family being as uninspiring as always. He was used to that. School was manageable, and best of all, he and Freddie were preparing for the next quest. Connor hoped it was going to happen soon. Where would Freddie's amazing map take them?

He peered through the travel agent's window at the glossy photographs. *We could end up anywhere*, he thought.

Connor used the window as a mirror to adjust his untidy black hair, but his heart skipped a beat when he saw his worst nightmare reflected in the glass. Five boys lined the kerb, all dressed in varieties of grey and black tracksuits.

Next to the dreaded Jasper came Paul, then Maz, Rowan and, finally, the smallest one, Kelvin. They stared across the road, like a band of villains in a movie stand-off. Connor saw Jasper's piercing blue eyes firmly fixed on him. Jasper was easily the tallest and toughest boy in their school year. He may have been surrounded by a bunch of hapless muppets, but he still scared Connor, especially when he was on his own without Freddie.

Connor felt his heart pounding. Things had

been quiet for a while since Freddie and Connor emerged triumphant from the summer's titanic battle. Connor had been attacked, but miraculously, it was the attackers who were left with the broken bones. There was no way Jasper would be happy to admit defeat. He would be after revenge.

Just then two buses blocked the five boys from view. By the time the second of them had passed, Connor's space on the pavement was empty. The gang frowned at each other, before silently turning and walking towards the shopping mall.

Connor was elated with the speed of his thought and action. *Maybe the diet was working already,* he thought. He caught his breath and wiped the sweat from his brow as the elderly woman in the sewing shop he was hiding in asked, "Are you after anything in particular?" Then she added hopefully, "There's a special on wool this week: three for two."

Connor smiled and nodded. "Thanks. But, um... I'm sorry – I've forgotten which colour my mum wanted."

He was back out on the street in time to see Jasper's most devoted follower, Kelvin, hobbling behind the others as they turned through the revolving doors of the mall. The skinny, slight boy jumped in at the third attempt, but still got knocked by the moving doors and everything stopped as a result. Connor could hear the laughter from the rest of the gang as he hurried on.

Turning the corner into Normandy Avenue, Connor immediately spotted Freddie's great-uncle Finnegan and great-aunt Kathleen on either side of Uncle Patrick, linked arm in arm with him. He gently led the ancient pair around the back of a huge removal van parked outside number 12, one house along from Freddie's. Connor caught their raised voices immediately. They shouted everything on account of their poor hearing.

His heart sank. Things were always a little hectic and unpredictable when the old couple were there. "Volatile" was how Mr Malone described them.

As Connor passed the removal van, he peered inside but was barged out of the way by a gruff man carrying a mattress. He arrived at Freddie's house just behind Uncle Patrick and the others, and was greeted with a hug and a kiss on each cheek by Mrs M.

"Ooh! There's my darlin'," she said. Freddie appeared from the hall, smiling a greeting with his brown eyes. He fist-bumped a hello. "Have you seen? We're getting new neighbours."

As they headed for the kitchen, Connor heard Finnegan shout to his wife, "The big fat boy's here as well, Kathleen. Make sure you get to the cake before he does." Mrs M quickly ushered the old man into the lounge, shooting an apologetic glance in Connor's direction.

Freddie put a hand on Connor's shoulder. "I'm sorry, mate. This'll happen more and more. They're going to come over two or three times a week from now on, Uncle Patrick says. They're not so good on their own anymore. We've got a family summit this evening when Dad's back from work to sort things out, but we've got ages to go till then."

There were already loud Irish voices coming from the lounge, which suddenly amplified as Mrs M emerged to put on the kettle.

"I should make yourselves scarce, boys. Finn's in one of his argumentative moods. I'm sorry for his rudeness, Connor. You're a darlin' boy and I wouldn't change a hair on your head."

Connor was finally able to relax in the serene surroundings of Freddie's bedroom, complete with a pint of orange squash and a plate of biscuits. As always, his eyes were drawn to the wonderfully illustrated antique map of the world on the wall to the right of Freddie's desk. The map was incredible. It smelled of spice stalls in foreign lands and its paint sparkled and glittered whether light shone on it or not. This was the mysterious magical gateway to Freddie's adventures.

Squeals of excitement erupted from next-door's garden. Connor looked down to see twin boys tearing after a plastic football. They looked about eight years old and were shouting excitedly to someone in the house. Connor pulled a face.

"Bit noisy."

"Well, I'm used to that around here," Freddie smiled. "C'mon, let's get to work."

Freddie picked up the book he and his best friend were compiling to help them on the next adventure. It had four pages devoted to each language they might possibly encounter. Freddie knew that he had been lucky that so many people in Nepal had spoken English, so he wanted to be fully prepared next time. They had already listed emergency phrases, friendly greetings and vital words in French, Spanish, Italian, Russian and German.

"TA DA! Portuguese! My Auntie Cheryl helped me. She had a Portuguese boyfriend once," said Connor proudly.

"Great, thanks."

"You mean *obrigado*!"

"What?"

"Portuguese for 'thank you'. *Obrigado* for boys, *obrigada* for girls."

Freddie smiled and began listing the new words.

Connor finished dictating the Portuguese *and* the plate of biscuits, then Freddie fired up his battered laptop and returned to researching the Greek vocabulary he was working his way through.

"I think something's going to happen soon. It just feels—"

"Well I'm ready to *rumble!*" said Connor, imitating a well-known sports commentator and making Freddie laugh. "Not a *stomach* rumble!" he added with a grin.

Freddie picked up a small tin. "Uncle Patrick's been collecting different currencies for me – odd coins from his work trips. I told him it was my new hobby. He's always off round the world doing... whatever job he does!"

Connor nodded. "Cool."

No one had ever established Uncle Patrick's exact career and Freddie thought his uncle enjoyed the sense of mystery it created. "I'm an international unicorn salesman!" was the latest answer he'd given to his nephew.

As Connor stood by the window staring down at next-door's garden, Freddie gazed at the map. The sense of anticipation was now so acute he could almost grasp it. He felt the map calling to him. But they had to get on with the notebook. Knowing what problems he'd had with his teeth, Connor looked up the Greek for 'dentist', 'filling', 'abscess' and 'anaesthetic', all things he'd recently experienced, whilst Freddie wrote down the translations. He stopped and stared at the map.

Sensing Freddie's trepidation, Connor said,

"I'll be with you next time to help and…" His voice tailed off. Freddie nodded and smiled.

"Thanks, mate. It'll be great. I really don't want to go by myself again. It's too difficult. I bet we'll be a fantastic team."

Freddie was doing his best to look positive, but secretly he was worried. The previous attempt to include Connor had not gone well, with Connor ending up half embedded in brickwork whilst Freddie was away.

Connor stayed quiet. He felt the butterflies in his stomach turning into something else: dread. The fear of failure. Failure to even enter the vortex successfully. He doubted he was small enough to go through the map. And even if he did end up actually entering the portal, what if he somehow sabotaged the whole mission? Or even worse, what if he messed up so badly that the pair of them could never return?

To take his mind off this unthinkable possibility, and although it was nearly lunchtime, he opened an emergency packet of chocolate wafers from the rucksack he'd hidden at the back of Freddie's wardrobe.

Freddie went downstairs for more drinks. As Connor waited for his return, he gazed at Nepal. At first he thought he was seeing things, but right there on the map a small dot appeared and started to grow before his very eyes. Then a shape emerged, getting stronger, clearer and larger, until it was about five centimetres tall. Then it started moving and in a few seconds it had formed perfectly into a shaggy, long-limbed yeti. It turned, smiled and waved at Connor, before fading and disappearing again. Connor opened his mouth in amazement. He shouted urgently, "Freddie!"

He looked back at the map and the yeti was gone, but suddenly a squirt of water shot out straight into his face. It was like being hit by a water pistol. Then again. It was coming from Niagara Falls. What was happening? The Falls sent out two more jets and Connor touched his hand to his face and watched as water trickled down his palm.

"Freddie, come quick!" he shouted again. He was petrified the map was about to pull him through on his own. A breeze ruffled his hair. He traced the source and saw the painted head of Neptune at the bottom left of the map. He normally directed his swirling breath at ships and galleons, but he now turned towards the room and a gobsmacked Connor. A blast of freezing cold air shot from the bearded sea god's mouth, blasting Connor in the face, before he winked and turned back to blowing up storms on the map.

Connor's mouth was dry from fear, but it was fear mixed with wonder. What was coming next?

His eyes were dragged to North Africa. Three perfect pyramids erupted from the map with a deep rumble, piercing the beautiful parchment. Dust and grit swirled around them, twinned with a giant clap of thunder as the Great Sphinx emerged from the cascading sand. It roared so loudly that Connor shot back across the room on the wheeled chair.

The other amazing apparitions faded and vanished almost as suddenly as they had first appeared, but the pyramids and the Sphinx remained.

Freddie returned and gasped at the sight of Connor pressed against the wall opposite the map, with a stunned look of wonder on his face. He looked frozen. Neptune's cold breath had blown his hair back as if he'd been riding a motorbike at a hundred miles an hour with no helmet on through a snowstorm. He had ice all over his face and hair that was cracking and falling off in tiny shards. Then Freddie saw Egypt's ancient monuments quite clearly poking out of the map. He blinked. Neither boy spoke for a second or two, until Connor, his eyes twinkling with excitement, said in the most normal voice he could manage considering he was nearly frozen, "I think I know where we're going on our next adventure."

Nodding in the direction of Egypt, he smiled as a melting icicle fell off his nose onto the carpet.

Chapter 2

"Egypt?" Freddie said, incredulously, mopping up the ice with his swimming towel.

Connor nodded firmly. "Yep, it's either there or Niagara Falls. Or it's a cruise to watch Neptune blow ships round the Antarctic." Connor tried to make Freddie laugh and failed.

"But we don't know anything about Egypt; the language, the money, the—"

"It's all right. We can look stuff up. Don't worry, I can help," Connor said with supreme confidence.

"But what if it's a red herring?"

"It felt pretty real to me."

There was silence for a moment, then Freddie nodded.

"No, you're right. The map must be trying to tell us something."

Freddie suddenly realised something else. It made him feel good. Really good. He realised he had faith and trust in the map. After all, he was its custodian and the map was his guide. And now, it also felt like his friend. What was even better was that it seemed happy to include Connor. Plus, it had given them a big clue.

Freddie's gentle smile returned.

"Clean yourself up and let's get down to it."

His laptop had only five per cent battery left, and was behaving erratically, so Freddie started it charging whilst Connor sorted out his hair. Then they raced downstairs for the encyclopedia in the lounge.

Finnegan and Kathleen had been whisked away for lunch by Uncle Patrick and a relative tranquillity had descended on the house.

Freddie took a deep breath. "I think we need some fresh air." Then he whispered, "And Mum can't hear us outside."

He led Connor to the bottom of the garden whilst the noise from next door continued sporadically. Despite the odd screech, Freddie and Connor settled down on the grass with drinks and the huge reference book.

Freddie chuckled. "You remember Finlay's christening, when Uncle Patrick fell in the hedge? At the end of his speech he raised his glass and toppled straight backwards."

Connor laughed and glanced at the considerable hole in the foliage. "Yeah and he didn't spill a drop of his beer!"

"Dad said it was a baffling feat of advanced physics, combined with Olympic gold-medal gymnastics."

Connor giggled. "He just lay there for ages, drinking and posing for photos. Don't reckon the hedge will ever recover; there's still a massive hole!"

The autumn sun was still quite strong and the boys quickly turned the pages of the heavy book to find the section on Egypt. The shouting started up again from the new neighbours. Freddie was about to suggest they retreat inside when their world changed again.

A cheap, orange football bounced off the top of Connor's head, making him spill his drink over himself and the precious encyclopedia.

All of a sudden a girl strode confidently through the gap in the hedge as if she owned the place.

Freddie took in the leggings, denim skirt, red football shirt and leather bomber jacket, then the face and hair. He looked over at Connor, who wore the expression of someone about to be hit by a truck.

She was very pretty, about their own age, and she had blue hair: a large chunk of bright, wavy blue on the left, with spiky blonde hair on the right-hand side. Whoever she was, she picked up the plastic football, turned and stared at them.

Connor let out an involuntary gasp and felt himself shrink. The girl cast a critical eye over them both. Freddie felt like an intruder in his own garden.

The girl frowned.

"What's wrong with you two? Never seen a football before?" With that, she expertly volleyed the ball just over the hedge to the two grateful boys on the other side.

Freddie couldn't think of anything to say, and another glance at Connor told him that his friend's power of speech was long gone. Why could some girls do that to you?

"Who are you then?" she demanded. "S'pose I'd better know who lives next door. Can either of you speak?" She took a step towards them.

Connor felt himself wriggling backwards on the grass, now soggy with the spilled drink. He watched as Freddie stood to greet her, but he stumbled slightly on Connor's moving leg, spilling yet more liquid over his friend and the book. Connor seemed oblivious and raised his eyes, daring to take another look.

Although not tall, she was compact and strong looking. She looked like she would be really good at PE. She had sapphire-blue eyes and long dark lashes.

"Wow, you two are random!" she said. "Have you never seen a *girl* before? Shall I come back when you've learned to hold drinks and stand up properly?"

"Hel – Hello, I'm Freddie. Freddie Malone. I live here. This is my best frie—"

"Ah! One of them speaks. We've just moved here coz Mum's got a new job. My name's Ruby and my brothers are Archie and Henry. They're twins. You'll see plenty of them when they come to get our ball back. We'll be doing penalties later if you want to have a go. You two both look like you'd be rubbish at football though."

"Thanks, err, maybe tomorrow. We've got some stuff to do, me and Con—"

"'Stuff', eh? Very mysterious. Well, you'd better get on with your *'stuff'* then. See ya." And with that she spun round and disappeared back through the hedge.

There was a silence as Freddie helped Connor up. He still appeared dumbstruck by Ruby's intrusion.

They trudged to the kitchen, where Connor tried to dry the spilled drink on his jumper with a tea towel, but succeeded only in making things worse. Freddie tried to mop at the wet pages of the book with kitchen roll.

"It needs drying out properly in the airing cupboard. Just separate the pages, so they don't all get stuck together, eh?" said Mrs M.

Just as it looked like some kind of calm might descend, Finnegan and Kathleen returned, arguing with Uncle Patrick about the quickest way to get back from the pub where they'd had lunch.

"As if it matters," sighed Freddie. The boys retreated upstairs, where Connor remained planted by Freddie's bedroom window, reporting on movements next door.

A few minutes later, Mr M returned from work and it was family summit time, so Connor had to go home. The boys made a plan to speak later, then he made a swift exit before Finnegan could call him fat again.

Freddie sat at the top of the stairs and did his best to follow the discussion below.

"It's no problem to us, feeding you, but don't you want to be independent in a nice little flat with a warden, y'know, if you need help with anything?" Freddie's mum suggested.

Then Mr M talked about money.

"If you sell that big old draughty place and buy a cosy, warm little flat, you can use the extra money to go on some holidays, buy a few luxuries for your old age, like—"

"What? I can't hear a word you're saying, Declan. You always talk so quietly," shouted Kathleen. Freddie had to grin because it sounded like his dad was yelling at the top of his voice over the tannoy at a football stadium.

Freddie joined them for dinner. The meal dragged on and eventually he made his excuses and went to his room to immerse himself in all things Egyptian: geography, history, anything! But his computer was playing up again and it kept freezing.

Soon, he heard Finnegan's raised voice climbing the stairs en route to the bathroom. "I don't care what you do. You're just trying to get rid of us. We're a problem and you've all had enough. I can see what you're up to. You just want our money!" he growled. Freddie's heart sank. He had so wanted the discussion to go well.

The bathroom door slammed shut and his great-uncle Finnegan rattled the lock. Fed up with his failing laptop, Freddie sat down on his bed and for the first time in hours there was finally a complete silence.

It lasted about eight seconds.

Suddenly, sparks of electricity shot out of the plug sockets and his computer flickered, then died, leaving a black screen. His radio sparked up with a random football commentary and the bedroom lights began pulsing. Freddie felt a surge of terror, anticipation, dread and excitement all at once. He was about to be called somewhere far away.

He dived towards the wardrobe, grabbed his rucksack and texted Connor.

SORRY GOT TO GO. F

Then it all started. The choirs rang out, the radio screamed '*goal!*', dramatic film music blared, jumbled with politicians' grand speeches, all overlapping and mashed up.

Freddie stared at the map, scared out of his wits. Could he do all this again? He'd often heard his dad say that the second time you do something is the hardest. Freddie hadn't understood back then, but now, sitting on the end of his bed, clutching his rucksack, he knew exactly what his father meant.

He glanced around the room, feeling the gradual increase in atmospheric pressure and trying to block out the noise. Then, with a searing flash the map seemed to burst into life. All over it, trains, planes, ships and animals started to move. The relief of the mountain ranges sprang up from the surface and he could see the great ocean swells and currents as they surged towards waiting shorelines.

The music, lights, voices and turbulence all increased as he felt his eyes being drawn to Egypt. The country on the map grew until it filled his entire vision. A huge blue river ran from the bottom to the top of the country, branching out like a tree as it neared the sea. It was the great river Nile. One second the mighty waterway was the static cobalt blue of the paint on the map, the next it was alive with boats and barges. Freddie swore he could smell it, his senses were overloaded but his nose could definitely pick out the aroma of cooked fish.

Then the map split apart by a city called Thebes, and the room began to shake. His clothes, books and just about everything except the furniture started to revolve and swirl in the gathering maelstrom caused by the rush of air from the vortex. Freddie held on tight to his bed, wanting desperately to know what the coming adventure held, but not quite daring to let go of his own familiar world. The word 'Thebes' dissolved and 'Waset' replaced it, before it, too, disappeared in a sudden gust of wind.

A flying book, caught up in the swirling chaos knocked his phone from his hand. "No! I need that for photos," he shouted. He tried to grab it back from the whirlwind. Then, as the mesmerising show of flashing lights and noise reached an earsplitting crescendo, his grip on the bed was broken and he began to hurtle towards the opening chasm in the map. A deafening sound like icebergs splintering filled his ears, as the hole in the map widened to allow him through. If he'd forgotten to pack anything, it was too late now.

He was on his way and nothing could stop him!

Chapter 3

The split in the map ran vertically up the river Nile. It was so realistic it felt like the bedroom would flood. Although Freddie was terrified, he tried to look for clues. He could easily pick out the word 'Karnak', but then a temple with huge pillars engulfed the word in front of his disbelieving eyes. The letters dissolved and were swept away as if they were grains of sand in a typhoon.

As a hundred trumpets sounded, he flew through the bedroom wall and into the mayhem beyond. He turned to look back towards his room through the closing fissure, and thought he saw the door swing open and someone enter, but the vortex pulled him away on his journey.

The tunnel was the same as last time: a greyish-purple twisting tube, like the inside of a giant garden worm, with pulsing plasma walls on which huge cinema-screen-sized portals rushed past, leading to hundreds of possible destinations. But they were all in a different order from before. Some even seemed like scenes from the future.

He passed one he recognised. The trench from a First World War battlefield flashed by, with what looked like an older version of Jasper leading a group of men in an attack. Freddie was buffeted against the wall opposite, which started his body spinning, as letters and numbers in different colours, shapes and languages seemed to zip through him as if he wasn't there. Freddie gasped as the words *odontiatros*, *apostima* and *plirosi* flew into his mouth. Quite apt really as they were the Greek words for dentist, abscess and filling!

Then came the portal with the guillotine. As he roared past, a woman with a pipe in her mouth celebrated another execution. There were grey portals too. Freddie guessed that meant they were now closed and inaccessible. There were dozens of them, scattered amongst the still-live destinations. *Who had entered all these other places? Who had been there before him?* He bounced harshly off the walls around a curve in the tunnel. He clutched the rucksack and felt the first hint of the momentum beginning to slow down.

The poem 'If—', his homeward mantra – the way for him to conjure up the vortex when he needed to return home — sounded about him, but the verses were not in the right order. Separate lines and different voices overlapped each other amidst the hundreds of other sounds.

Just when Freddie was beginning to feel calmer, dozens of semi-transparent cloaked figures surrounded him and he felt an entirely new terror. This was something different. Huge hoods covered their features, and ghostly, harsh whispers emanated from them. They weren't harming him though, despite their menacing appearance. They moved like frenzied eels, contorting in a hectic dance around and through Freddie. He was beginning to accept their presence and feel almost protected by them, until two fuller figures, firmer in outline than the rest, brushed past, and for a second Freddie could feel their touch. The smaller, leading apparition turned and headed aggressively straight back towards Freddie, but then the bigger chasing shape intercepted and drove the attacker away. The interceptor turned and saluted Freddie.

In an instant, all the cloaked figures completely disappeared and Freddie came to an inglorious halt, spreadeagled against the side frame of a portal. The tempest around him died down.

What was that all about? He was shaken by what had just happened. *If only Connor were here.*

It came as a massive shock to realise that instead of the vortex being his own personal time link with

34

the past and future, it seemed that others – ghosts, demons or whatever they were – used it as well.

Freddie gathered his strength and focused on the portal. The time code was spinning wildly. *Hang on.* The numbers were going backwards, not forwards. Previously he'd watched decades pass in a matter of seconds, from 1989 to 2019. But now the digital clock was losing years. One moment it was 2250 and by the time he felt compelled to enter, the year was reading 1328. The time code froze as he stepped through the plasma opening with the numbers set and no longer flashing red and black.

As he stared back at his entry point, a stray capital 'B' and 'C' floated down and a shiver of excitement coursed through Freddie.

He must be in ancient Egypt in 1328 BC. He had travelled back at least 3,300 years, maybe more. He would work out the exact number later, but for now all he could think about was the searing heat he felt as he surveyed his new surroundings. His skin reacted at once to the immense change in temperature and he immediately started to sweat.

Freddie found himself in a verdant glade, surrounded by dense, chest-high grasses and bulrushes, with patches of thick undergrowth and towering palm trees providing plenty of cover from prying eyes. His first thought was *How will I ever find this place again to get home?*

He needed to climb up high. He spotted a rocky outcrop a hundred metres or so ahead of him that he felt he could easily use as a marker for the portal. Taking a deep breath and wishing himself luck, he set off towards the landmark, counting his steps carefully and trying to stay in a straight line. After seventy-five paces he came upon a small wooden pen that contained a beautiful, cream-coloured calf and its huge-horned, brown-and-white mother. The calf nudged Freddie's arm and nuzzled his hand. Freddie tickled him above his nose and tore up a clump of long grass, which the grateful animal devoured messily. He repeated this service twice before telling himself to move on. Feeding a grateful calf was not the reason he had been called to ancient Egypt, he was absolutely sure of that!

With a final stroke of the animal's nose, Freddie walked around the pen, making a mental note of his direction, as he set off towards a distinctive-looking palm tree which stood near a crack in the base of the outcrop. Its trunk was split near the top, creating two identical heads. As he scaled the rock, he turned and could clearly see his path through the disturbed grass. The intense sun was really beginning to prickle his fair Irish skin, so Freddie was pleased he and Connor had thought to pack sun cream.

He looked ahead and saw the path he needed to take back to the portal. It lined up perfectly with a distinctive mountain peak in the distance. He studied the path and then sketched it in his notebook. *Great, at least I can find my way home,* he thought. Confident of his escape route he began to relax.

In the middle distance was a wide and majestic river. This had to be the Nile. It was covered with a mass of ancient-looking sailing boats of all shapes and sizes, all travelling in different directions. Several much larger barge-type boats, which had huts roofed with straw two thirds of the way along from the bow, were sailing in straight lines up and down the river, adding to the chaos of the smaller craft trying to dodge them.

As he studied the terrain, Freddie noticed a wide strip, maybe one or two kilometres deep on each bank of the river, which was a lush, dark green. Other than the glade in front of him, every other square metre seemed to be cultivated and was growing fruit, nuts, or what looked like wheat or barley. Then, as if someone had used a giant craft knife to cut an outline, the green changed abruptly and completely to the golden yellow of sand and the grey and brown of rocks and dust. The river spread its life-giving powers for a short distance, but was no match for the endless miles of barren desert that dominated on all sides.

"Wow!" said Freddie. He started to feel the sweat stick his T-shirt to his skin. It certainly made a change from being freezing and unable to breathe properly as he had been in Nepal. *Why always these extremes?* he wondered.

Diagonally left across the river was a magnificent cluster of shrines forming what looked like a huge temple complex. It had dozens of pillars and in the centre were two rows of six even stouter columns, at least twice as tall as the others. It was enormous.

Around the temple was a large town of tightly packed mud dwellings. There were several wider roads in the distance, lined with beautiful villas and statues. Settlements had sprung up all around in a sprawl of complicated streets and alleys.

To his right, the river flowed into the hazy distance with huts scattered on stilts by the waterside. It was all surrounded by fields of oxen ploughing, fruit ripening and grapes growing fat and juicy. He was close enough to hear the sporadic shouts as workers toiled nearby in the sunshine, farming the rich, black, fertile soil.

Freddie turned his back to the river and was amazed by what he saw. Where the green fields gave way to the desert, there lay five more temples all of different sizes and styles, forming an irregular line in front of some quite big hills beyond.

Slightly to the left and closest to Freddie were the two largest statues he had ever seen. Two 20-metre-high seated Egyptian pharaohs guarded the entrance to a very spacious and well-laid-out complex. Freddie desperately wanted to see the giants close up.

What lay ahead on this adventure? Why was he here? He felt the need to explore rather than take part in any heroics just at the moment.

But how would he possibly blend in and communicate with what was obviously ancient Egyptian society? He wished he'd had more time to look up facts before the map had opened.

A series of piercing trumpet calls came from a walled garrison by the river, and Freddie's attention was diverted to a parade of chariots that emerged through its high gates and travelled at speed towards the temples.

Hundreds of soldiers ran in well-ordered ranks behind the dust-spewing chariots. Freddie couldn't miss this spectacle. He needed a better view, and some shade.

He quickly changed into his white PE shorts and T-shirt and swapped his trainers for sandals. Then he shinned up the tree and stowed his rucksack safely in the crook of the two-headed palm where no one could see it, and made his way eagerly to the edge of the dense cover.

Whatever was about to happen, he didn't want to miss it.

Chapter 4

Freddie moved quickly to the edge of a huge, dusty, scrubby arena the size of several football pitches. It was surrounded by a deep water-filled ditch on the other three sides. The thick vegetation, where Freddie was hiding, provided boundary enough, and four narrow bridges crossed at different points. The trumpets sounded again and twenty chariots, each pulled by two horses, kicked up enormous clouds of dust as they arrived and lined up in front of some musicians. Freddie felt exhilarated by it all.

The charioteers took a while to get their skittish charges under control and to manoeuvre them into position. All were richly decorated and held a single soldier or nobleman. Once settled, attendants supplied them with drinks and food, whilst other servants held the horses firmly in place.

Another fanfare blared and a magnificent golden chariot pulled by two horses covered in leopard skins emerged through the settling dust clouds. Sunlight glinted off the occupant and the carriage's golden frame. From the temple opposite, a procession of what looked like priests and drummers walked between the two stone pharaohs and snaked their way over a bridge and on to the flat scrubland. They halted before the golden chariot.

In complete contrast to the rugged stature of the men in the surrounding carriages, peering over the guard rail and holding the reins as tightly as if his life depended on it, was a small, frightened-looking boy of about Freddie's age dressed entirely in gold.

The priests bowed and lay flat on the ground with outstretched arms, whilst an elderly man in flowing white robes, also with a leopard skin hanging down his back, walked forwards. He wore an enormous blue headdress, which contained something that caught the sun and sparkled. He approached the slight, golden figure in the carriage.

A short ritual took place. Chants, trumpet blasts, and gesticulations were followed by the sprinkling of liquid over everyone and everything. Then the ceremony came to an abrupt end as the musicians, priests and attendants stopped mid-tune, gathered up their long, flowing robes and made an undignified and hasty exit.

Freddie was mesmerised. What was about to unfold? Unseen drums began striking a rather sinister beat somewhere to Freddie's left. As the last of the fleeing priests hurried between the protective stone giants, a dreadful noise started up close by. A wondrously decorated priest on horseback led a beautiful young cream calf into the arena. A horrible feeling hit hard in Freddie's stomach.

"Oh no! Please, no!"

The beast was led to a spot a hundred metres in front of Freddie. The small animal tested the air with a twitching nose.

From Freddie's right, a shrill and fearsome protest split the air as the calf's mother, the brown-and-white cow, pulled a dozen men in her wake. They had ropes round her, but still she struggled to get to her stranded calf. Recognising its mother, the calf began a plaintive reply and pulled on its leash, but it was no match for the tight grip of the priest. As the calf's fearful notes and its mother's terrifying warning reached a crescendo, the priest raised a sword. It glinted in the sun for a second and descended in an arc to silence the noise.

Nothing stirred, even the cow fell quiet and stopped pulling. The priest let go of his rope and the dead calf sagged to the ground. The ropes were dropped from the mother, who slowly approached her calf, sniffing the ground before nuzzling her son. She raised her head and uttered a long mournful cry, her anguished gaze directed at the priest, who was riding away fast towards the temple.

Freddie's face was contorted in distress. "What else can they possibly do?" he whispered. It wasn't only leopards that were in danger in this part of the world, then.

The horses of the charioteers were restless. Dust rose from their impatient hooves now their handlers had disappeared.

Then the tension increased again as dozens of frisky bullocks were forced over each bridge. Their hooves thudded and clattered wildly over the wooden boards. They gathered together into a single mass, and looked nervously around for clues as to what the future held.

The sun glinted again off metal, this time unsheathed by the charioteers. Some drew swords; others held powerful bows.

Attendants tied their horses' reins securely around their waists, so they could steer their charges using their hips, allowing them both hands free for their weapons.

Suddenly, twenty chariots and their drivers were hurtling towards the stunned bullocks, who scattered seeking an escape. Most turned opposite to the advancing tide but the first swords easily picked off several stragglers that tried to run out to the side.

The charioteers expertly steered their charges with a turn of the hips, whilst firing their arrows at speed. Their skill and precision was frightening.

Freddie saw the flash of the swords, the fury of the chase and the pain of the injured and dying. One chariot and driver ploughed straight into the deep ditch as the bullock it was following turned at the last second. Neither horse nor man emerged. Two other chariots lay overturned with their drivers trampled by fleeing hooves or wooden wheels.

Freddie stared open-mouthed at the madness, cursing the map and Uncle Patrick for bringing him here to witness this dreadful spectacle. He became aware that amongst the melee of dust and carnage, standing in his chariot and not party to the slaughter in front of him, was the golden boy in his golden carriage. His frame looked slightly contorted, leaning over to his left with his eyes lowered, tightly clasping the reins of his fretting horses.

A tall, shaven-headed man, finely dressed, began tying the horses' reins around the golden boy's waist through the open back of the chariot. He tested them roughly, then produced a heavy, golden sword that he thrust into the boy's hand. He barely looked strong enough to lift the weapon, let alone fight with it.

Next, the tall man signalled, and a blast of trumpets and crash of drums called a final halt. By now, every bullock had been sacrificed, and the remaining charioteers made their way to the far side of the arena. They turned and lined up opposite Freddie, dismounted and clasped each others forearms in celebration of the honour they believed they had delivered to the gods.

Freddie was utterly disgusted. He had never seen anything so one-sided and horrible in his life. He wanted to flee back to the portal and escape.

The only thing that stopped him doing so was a distraught bellow from the one remaining animal alive in the arena. The original cow still stood guarding the tiny body of her calf. Again she nuzzled the dead animal, hoping beyond hope that it would stir.

The drums struck up once again, increasing in tempo.

The man accompanying the golden chariot slapped his hand on the leopard skin covering the nearest horse's flank, and the team leaped forward into a frenzied gallop.

As the horses thundered round the arena, their golden cargo bucked and swayed perilously from side to side. Suddenly, as they swerved around one of the dead animals, the chariot was tipped dangerously onto one wheel. As it crashed back down to the ground, the boy lost his footing and was thrown backwards out of the chariot. One rein snapped, but he was still tied to the horses by the other and was being dragged along the rough ground.

Freddie gasped.

Nobody moved.

Not one of the assembled charioteers, nobility,

officials or priests came to the rescue of the golden boy. It seemed almost as though they all expected this to happen. Freddie could not stand by and let this boy suffer. It felt like he was a glorified golden sacrifice.

The boy was bouncing along the ground, dragged like a rag doll, but he managed somehow to wield the sword and sever the remaining rein that bound him. It danced wildly away with the speeding chariot and the boy skidded to a painful stop in the rock-strewn dust.

The world seemed to stand still. With a feeling Freddie instantly recognised, he suddenly knew his calling and the reason for his being in this ancient land. His mission was crystal clear now.

As the cow side-stepped her dead calf, lowered her horns and pawed menacingly at the ground to assess her stricken enemy, Freddie felt a calm envelop him. He broke cover from the treeline and ran towards the fallen boy.

At the same time, the mother cow prepared herself to charge. She was momentarily distracted by the sight of a small, mousey-haired boy in sandals and PE kit running towards her intended target, but seemed to use the interruption as a spur to get there before him.

Freddie hurtled breathlessly towards the boy, sprinting for all he was worth. He swooped low and picked up the heavy sword in his final few steps, before planting himself firmly between the boy and the charging cow.

He suddenly froze. *What am I he doing? How can I stop the charge of this mighty beast?*

In a flash, he remembered Uncle Patrick at a family picnic shooing away cattle that had threatened to trample the food-laden blanket. Freddie made himself as big as possible and shouted with all his might, as the cow charged on towards them both. Wielding the sword around his head and shoulders, he shouted and began advancing on the beast, who skidded to a confused halt in a storm of dust.

Freddie tried to catch his breath but all he took in was a lungful of dirt. As the cloud cleared, panting beast faced panting boy and the world stood still. Their eyes locked and Freddie could see that the animal had no more fight left in her. The strength of purpose that Freddie had demonstrated seemed to impose a control over the situation. The cow backed away, before silently sagging to the floor under the hail of arrows from the advancing foot soldiers. With her eyes locked on Freddie, she collapsed and lay shattered on the ground. "Noooo!" came Freddie's dusty scream.

He sank to his knees, using the sword to stop himself falling forward. Freddie felt extremely faint and he crashed to the ground as the foot soldiers formed a tight circle about the two boys with spears, swords and bows facing out.

It's a bit late for that, thought Freddie as he turned and found the frightened and thankful eyes of the golden boy, who lay bleeding and helpless on the ground near him. The boy made a slight nod of the head in Freddie's direction. Freddie replied with his own nod of understanding.

The soldiers in front of Freddie broke rank and a powerfully built older man strode through the gap. He carried a heavy ornamental-looking spear and exuded authority and importance. He had an icy, fixed glare like a laser trained firmly on Freddie, as he walked to the side of the badly injured golden boy. They exchanged a few words, before the important man made a weak bow. Then he took five purposeful paces towards Freddie and, for some extraordinary reason, he struck him hard on the side of his head with the base of his spear.

Chapter 5

"He did what?" spluttered Connor, showering himself with crumbs.

"The next thing I knew I was lying on a funny bed thing in a beautiful room with servants fanning me."

Freddie had been back from Egypt since 3 am. He'd checked the date and time on his recharged laptop, just after he'd flopped back through the map, which magically healed itself, as did the wall behind it.

He'd been gone for just five hours. It was impossible to believe he had somehow packed nearly two months of adventure into three hundred minutes.

Now safely sitting in his garden with Connor, it was only a day after Ruby had appeared through the hedge, and the explosive family summit.

Connor was taking his disappointment at missing out remarkably well. He had half predicted it would happen and understood it wasn't anything Freddie could control. That disappointment, however, was now completely replaced by fascination at the tale Freddie was relating.

"Sorry, carry on. I won't interrupt. You were on a funny bed, being fanned by servants?"

Freddie nodded.

"I woke up wearing a white linen top and kilt thing called a shendyt. There were three daybeds in a triangle shape facing each other, with big, golden, carved animal heads on the posts in the middle of this huge room in the palace. It took the golden boy ages to recover, because he was really bruised and cut up. He already had a badly injured foot from birth, which made him limp, and he walked with a stick.

"He had a pet hunting dog called Dedu, who was always curled up at his feet. He was waist-high and ginger – and luckily he seemed to like me straight away.

"But listen, Connor, I was so shocked when I found out whose life I'd saved! Can you guess?"

Connor shrugged. "Well, the son or grandson of the king?"

"No. I had saved the life of the pharaoh himself,

'The King of the Two Lands' – that's Egypt – and not just any old king. I'd saved the life of the golden boy king himself, Tutankhamun."

"King Tutankhamun! You're joking me."

"No, I'm not, and he insisted we recuperate together in the palace. We made each other laugh because to start with we couldn't communicate except by sign language. One of the first things he taught me was to call him Kha."

"But how old was he?"

"Same as me and you, thirteen!"

"Thirteen!"

"He'd been king since he was *nine*!" said Freddie, as Connor shook his head in wonder. "And get this, he was *married*!"

"Wha…?" Connor put both hands over his mouth to stop a snort. His eyes were wide with amazement.

"Kha's wife, Ankhesenamun – Ankha for short, well she's – she *was* – five years older than Kha. I know it sounds mad, Connor, but the most famous royal couple of all time were just like frightened kids really. They were surrounded by really powerful men who just wanted rid of them, so that they could rule Egypt instead.

"For the majority of the time, the three of us spent our days together, and it was awesome. We quickly got to trust each other and they helped me learn the language, with these tutors, Mitry and Paser.

"Mitry taught me swordsmanship, archery and how to dance. I wasn't so keen on the dance thing, but the archery and swordplay were great. Kha gradually joined in as he felt better, and was dead fast for someone who was injured and basically pretty disabled due to his foot. I could see how determined he was and his health, fitness and especially his smile grew every day.

"The other tutor, Paser, taught me language and hieroglyphics. I worked really hard and learned quickly."

"That's brilliant," said Connor.

"Yes, and I used to teach them little bits of English, which was really useful when we didn't want people to know what we were talking about. Like a spy language! I called it *Albanicus*, because English hadn't been invented yet, remember. The only trouble was, the better I spoke Egyptian, the more I had to invent a believable cover story for me being there." Freddie laughed. "In the end even *I* was convinced it was the truth."

"What did you tell them?" Connor prompted.

Freddie smiled distantly. "Well it was easy, really. Paser told me about all the other children of foreign emissaries. Every country had officials there, eager to keep in with Egypt. They were a superpower. Everyone assumed I was the son of an ambassador and I played along, explaining that I was from Albion, a far-off country on the other side of the world. My parents had been bringing gifts to the pharaoh but were shipwrecked on the Nile and I was separated from them in the water.

"As time went on Kha sent out scouts to search for two white-skinned emissaries, but they all returned empty-handed. I hated lying to people, but it was for the best. I could hardly tell them the truth."

"So, what about Ankha?" asked Connor, as casually as possible. "What did she look like?"

Freddie sat back and smiled. "Well, she was taller than Kha, and she had that shiny black hair, like the pictures of Cleopatra, with beads and jewels in it, at the sides and front – but not at the back. She'd never be able to sleep, it'd be like lying on boulders," Freddie laughed.

"Her skin was olive-coloured and smooth, but she wore tons of make-up, especially round her eyes. Even Kha had this black stuff slapped on. Kohl it's called. They tried it on me once, but I said it aggravated my skin." Freddie and Connor laughed.

"Ankha had two handmaidens, Nedjem and Kyky, who were about eighteen as well. They were devoted to her and fussed over her dresses and make-up and hair and stuff. When she laughed with Kha and me, her big, bright-green eyes lit up, and her face burst into smiles.

"Ankha was unbelievably clever and quick. She really cared about Kha and worried about him all the time, like an older sister looking out for a struggling younger brother.

"He walked with quite a limp and dragged his left foot. He had thick black hair and was striking to look at, with a long nose and darker skin than Ankha. He had huge brown eyes that were really friendly and warm when he was in no pain, and his first instinct was to laugh at things if he could. But when he was having a spasm or fit, Ankha would take charge. She would stroke his cheek and sing softly, cradling him until the seizure passed.

"When he came round he couldn't remember anything that had happened. I only saw it twice and it was always after he was really stressed by something.

"Only a few Egyptians ever met or even saw Kha, but the shock and, I guess, disappointment people showed was a difficult thing to watch. Paser told me that Kha was supposed to be a living god and immortal. He was the whole focus of their religion. Kha was supposedly related to Amun, the god of light. But when people met him, I could see the surprise in their eyes, however much they tried to disguise it. Kha could see it as well. He told me he *knew* he was just an ordinary boy, not a god. He didn't ask to be king. One day, when he was six, his mad dad died and that was it. King! Bingo!

"He didn't actually reign until he was nine, but he was married straight away to Ankha, because the country needed a stable royal dynasty, following years of chaos under his father, a guy called Akhenaten who was really strange and unpopular.

"Kha also had two very powerful advisors, called viziers, a bit like prime ministers. One was Horemheb, the head of the army. He was the thug who smashed me in the head. Kha went mad at him," Freddie continued. "So Horemheb made himself scarce for a bit. But that left us with this even more horrible man, called Ay. He was the man who slapped Kha's horses into action at the massacre.

"He was tall and about fifty, I guess, with a shaved head. He was really sinister. When he smiled, he only used his mouth – and he had black eyes, like a shark's. He just stared at you. Like dead eyes. He made me shiver. Ay treated Kha really badly and seemed to rule his life. Both he and Ankha just did as he told them, without question.

"Ay wanted to get rid of me immediately. He was disgusted that I'd got so close to them. Ankha kept saying that Ay wanted to inherit the throne for himself.

"Two or three times a day Ay would arrive from nowhere, to shove some papyrus under Kha's nose for his approval. When he was around, the whole atmosphere changed: the tutors disappeared into the shadows and the laughter stopped.

"When Ankha saw Ay, she just stared straight ahead. She reminded me of a doll, with a beautiful mask showing a blank face to the vizier. But when Ay looked at Ankha, well, I hated the way he stared at her. Everyone did.

"Ay reminded me of Jasper. Two peas from the same horrible pod, three-and-a-half thousand years apart. It just shows, you can be the king of the world's most powerful country and still be bullied. It's not just us, Connor." The pair sat in silence, then Freddie said, "I felt such a loyalty to them. They were like two beautiful birds trapped in a golden cage."

"Wow," Connor said. "Keep going, Freddie, please."

Chapter 6

As the massive scabs on Kha's arms and legs gradually healed, the two boys and the faithful hound, Dedu, explored further afield. Freddie had lessons in charioteering from Parennefer, the gigantic commander of the 'loyal guard', a small group of elite soldiers who would give their lives to protect their pharaoh.

The palace was laid out in gently descending steps down a slight hill, with the royal apartments at the top. The gardens were gradually turned into a racetrack as the boys created a challenging circuit, riding in a big basic chariot that easily held them and the dog. It even had a back bar, which Kha could lean on to take the pressure off his foot.

They got bolder and faster and had competitions, but if the daily pain Kha lived with became too much to bear, he would apologetically call for assistance and depart with Ankha, who would stroke his pain away and sing him to sleep. Freddie's admiration for this fragile but fiercely determined boy grew and grew.

When Kha was too ill, Freddie explored with Paser and Mitry, who told him about the architecture and history of various buildings and temples and about the religion and ceremony of the Two Lands.

One day, against Ay's wishes, Kha suggested they venture out of the palace disguised as young priests with distinctive blue headdresses. They rode far away from the luxurious confines of the palace of Amenophis III. It lay south of the magnificent line of temples Freddie had seen when he first arrived. In front of the palace gates lay a huge reservoir about 500 metres long. It was fed by several channels from the river and a series of special cranes called shadoofs lifted the water into irrigation ditches, which fed the palace and its gardens. Freddie marvelled at the clever system. He was living history with every step he took.

Left out of the main gates in front of them rose the smaller temples of Thutmose I and II, opposite the huge Temple of Amenhotep III, whose front gates were the Colossi of Memnon, the giant seated figures that Freddie at last could touch and marvel at.

"I wish I had my camera," he whispered as his hands stroked the beautifully carved stone giants. But it was no use regretting anything, he had to soak it all in so he could return and tell his tale.

In their priestly disguise, Freddie and Kha went about unchallenged. These were glorious, happy hours exploring as inquisitive 13-year-olds.

Driving south one day along the banks of the mighty Nile, they came across an elderly farmer who was struggling to draw water from the river by means of a shadoof. The levels were low at this time of the year and it was incredibly hard work. The shadoof had seen better days and was a little rickety, like the farmer himself.

It took a lot of strength to pull down the counterweighted end to lift the water-filled pouch up, and at the same time turn the upright post before depositing the water into the irrigation channel on top of the riverbank.

Freddie helped the old man heave the pouch out of the water and Kha, with a huge smile on his face, supervised the emptying of the contents.

For the best part of an hour, the boys sweated and toiled as they perfected their technique, realising it was best to only fill the pouch three quarters full. They sang a rhythmic chant the farmer taught them, about how workers were the real life-blood of Egypt, not the lazy pharaohs. With any other king, the farmer would have been arrested and executed, but Kha just roared with laughter.

Eventually all three collapsed exhausted. Parennefer and the guards who had watched with some amusement from a respectful distance, took over and made the job look easy. The farmer shared some rough bread with the boys after thanking them for all their help. Then he grew gradually quiet as it began to dawn on him that these were not two boy priests at all. With the titles that the soldiers used to address the darker boy, he eventually understood he was in the presence of the boy king of Egypt! He wept openly and flung himself face down in the mud at Kha's feet, begging for forgiveness. Kha graciously waved away the apology, even though the lyrics of the song had suggested taking all the pharaohs, viziers and officials and throwing them into the Nile to feed the hippos and crocodiles.

"Change the words," said Freddie. "Throw all the viziers in the river, but keep Lord Kha safe and well!"

It was agreed and the song was chanted again by them all incorporating the new lyrics. All, that is, except one of the guards: Rudjek, a short, squat man, with shifty eyes, and he viewed Freddie with barely-disguised suspicion as he continued to work the shadoof with the others. Freddie felt a shiver of dread as he realised that maybe not everyone in the guard could be trusted. He also felt a strange sensation that they were being watched from a distance, a feeling he'd had often since his arrival in Egypt.

Some days they took food and squeezed a laughing Ankha into the chariot. Kha closed his eyes, spread his arms out wide and let the onrushing air cool his perspiring brow. It gave him the feeling he was flying. They swam in a beautiful pond fed by the Nile. Nedjem and Kyky would travel ahead and lay out a feast under shady awnings, always having to shout at Dedu to leave the sweet honey cakes alone. But he was a very skilful thief and always managed to run off with some delicacy, and proudly sat just out of reach devouring his catch.

Kyky was always laughing and had a passion for tickling Freddie. Sometimes her husband, Kawab, would entertain everyone. He was a superb musician and played the harp, the flute and the lyre. Nedjem danced traditional steps in the shimmering afternoon heat to Kawab's beautiful songs, and the group relaxed in the wonderful safety of each other's company, well away from the palace and its corridors full of secrets and malice.

But on Horemheb's return from a mission on the Nubian border, he confirmed Ay's ruling and banned the royal couple from travelling unless accompanied by a hundred soldiers and ten chariots, which swiftly put an end to the freedom and fun of the trio.

Freddie had to be inventive, so when all the palace thought they were having an afternoon sleep, they would sneak out using the water conduit system that carried the precious filtered Nile water down through the centre of the palace in a series of shallow steps under the walls and floors, and through the gardens. Every few metres, little branch channels would take water to different areas and it was easily possible for a smallish teenager to travel considerable distances through the palace in the cool, shallow water underneath it. It was a small taste of freedom, and more about rebelling against the harsh regime of the viziers than anything else.

But the fun couldn't last, as Kha was now fully back to health and he had official duties to undertake – the most important of which was to inspect his own tomb.

It was not unusual, indeed it was expected, that a king or queen would visit their tomb as it was being built. Even the smallest tomb took two years to create, so work started as soon as the previous ruler was interred. When important people died, they were embalmed. After the embalming process was complete, seventy days after death, their treasures were amassed underground, along with food and offerings for the gods in the next life. It was no more troubling to the king than visiting any other official building.

For many centuries the rulers of Egypt had been buried in an area called the Valley of the Kings. Kha's father, Akhenaten, had been buried apart in the West Valley – *almost like a naughty pharaoh*, thought Freddie. So he was dismayed when the huge royal entourage bypassed the East Valley and continued on to the West Valley to begin their tour of inspection.

At the tomb entrance, there were blindfolded musicians playing, and priests and officials lined up opposite the workmen who were building the tomb. The workers stared at Kha. They'd been told he was a god, and here he was, just a boy. And a boy with severe physical difficulties as well. It wasn't what they had expected and Freddie felt the awkward and embarrassing silence. He started to shout, "Long live the Amun! Long live the god of life! Long live the king of the Two Lands!"

Everyone joined in and Ankha turned and smiled at Freddie, before Ay fixed his black eyes on him and shook his head. But he too had to join in for fear of standing out.

Kha jumped down, landing perfectly in the dust and called forward Paser, who produced a cloth bag. It was full of engraved medals that celebrated the building of the tomb. These were distributed by an overseer to the cheering workers, who each kneeled to show their loyalty.

Then, standing at the tomb entrance and using Freddie as a support, Kha turned to the gathering.

"I'm sure the god Amun has shown you the great plan for my journey to the next life. I know you work hard to complete the task. It is your job to work for the glory of Amun. I – his incarnation in this life – thank you for honouring both Amun and me. The next time I shall be in this place my eyes will have been shut for seventy days. My spirit will be ready to travel through the twelve stages of night towards Osiris. You will have helped make that journey possible. You are loyal and true. And your king, your pharaoh and your god thank you."

As the cheers rang out, the frail boy walked unaided a few metres into the tomb until, safely out of sight, he collapsed wearily against the wall. As Freddie handed him his walking stick, his face broke into a huge grin.

"You must write all my speeches," he whispered to Freddie with a grateful smile as Ankha joined them, and they descended deep into the mountainside.

A twelve-step staircase took them down into a long, sloping corridor. Then they helped Kha down a longer flight of torch-lit steps.

The temperature was dramatically cooler than outside, but the atmosphere was nonetheless cramped and claustrophobic. A thin, greasy-haired man pushed his way through the large number of people following.

"Lord Tutankhamun. Your gracious Royal Majesty, living image of Amun. He who calms and rules the Two Lands. He who propitiates the Cosmic Order and—"

"Yes, yes, get on with it!" boomed Horemheb, from behind in the packed tunnel. "You are using up the air of twenty men." There was a ripple of laughter.

The man continued his introduction. "I am Userhat, my Lord. I am assistant to Maya, the grand architect of your tomb. He is very ill and commands me in his absence to answer any questions regarding your final resting place."

Horemheb was now at the front of the crowd

following in the packed tunnel. "All right, the king heard you. Move your slimy carcass," he said. He was obviously a man more at ease in open spaces, not dark, packed, airless tombs.

"Thank you, Userhat," Kha said, politely. "I have no questions, but you will be summoned if I think of any." Sweeping past the assistant architect, the throng walked down the second sloping corridor to a square chamber, the smallest of three rooms recently excavated from the surrounding limestone and shale.

Only Kha and Ankha progressed further now, as Paser subtly stopped Freddie following into the large second room, the king's burial chamber, and beyond to the canopic chamber where his internal organs would be kept in jars after his death.

Kha had previously described how the body was embalmed after the removal of the internal organs. It had completely put Freddie off his supper that night, but Kha and Ankha thought it completely natural. The boy king reached across and with a smile threw Freddie's uneaten Nile perch to a grateful Dedu.

Freddie stood in silence, watching his two friends, arm in arm, circle the rooms and inspect the murals, which were outlined but not yet painted. Freddie wracked his brains trying to remember facts about Tutankhamun. He could remember that he had died young and although vast wealth was found with him, it was in a cramped, tiny place. But this place didn't feel tiny at all. Freddie surveyed the layout, memorising every detail.

A call was sounded to clear the tomb except for the high priest, Nibamon, and the royal astronomer and junior vizier, Khensuhotep. A ritual was to take place within the burial chamber with only the four of them present.

The slow process of everyone else filing out began. Freddie smiled at Kha and made his halting way towards the daylight. At the base of the second flight of steps, he saw Userhat pass a message on a piece of papyrus to Ay. The vizier then quickly moved on.

Out in the open again, the fierce sun beat down and people quickly dispersed. The workers had already set off for their village, Pa Demi, which lay south of the East Valley in the direction of the Nile. A shortcut could clearly be seen around the left shoulder of the mountain and a telltale trail of dust rose from their feet.

Freddie saw Userhat take the same path, then moments later, Ay followed. Freddie's eye's narrowed and he thought of the papyrus note. *Something's up*, he thought.

"Paser, I'm going to wait for the king and queen and travel back with them." Freddie thought this was a convincing fib.

"Very well, but find some shade. You will cook if you sit in this heat." As Paser drove off spitting stones and dust from the fast-turning wheels of his chariot, Freddie slipped away and took the path following Ay and Userhat. He quickly saw that they were now walking together, struggling up the tricky path about 250 metres ahead.

So what business did they have with each other? Freddie knew he needed to find out for the safety of his friends.

Chapter 7

Freddie had to hold back as he reached the top of the short, tough climb so as not to alert his quarry. The vizier and his oily companion had reached the East Valley floor and were making for a tiny opening in the rocks. As soon as they disappeared from view, Freddie took a direct route down the scree surface to save time, sliding perilously down several sections of jagged, loose stone before reaching the same tiny cavity in the hillside.

Freddie gathered his nerve and edged his way down sixteen steps into the darkness, and then along a sloping corridor. There was just the last of the spilled sunlight from the entrance to help him see his way. Feeling his way along the wall, he tiptoed silently, as close as he dared, towards the hushed voices. He could make out shadows on the walls of a small chamber ahead. Two figures were lit by a single flaming torch, which created a spooky shadow dance on the far wall.

Freddie had to get nearer to find out what was going on. He hid behind the left side of the doorway, and when the men moved to the right from the first chamber, they climbed down into a room beyond. Freddie peered round to see the layout. This was also a tomb under construction, but nothing like the grand subterranean rooms he had just seen. Two small chambers were directly ahead of him, with a low doorway linking them. They were both smaller than his kitchen at home and he felt confined, even with bare walls and no furniture. To the right, off the first room, a head-high gap led to a third space, which Ay's torch now illuminated. It was about a metre below the first room and was almost completely filled with the stone base of a sarcophagus which Ay and Userhat awkwardly navigated as they circled the base and went right again, to yet another room hidden from Freddie's view.

His eyes were now accustomed to the dim, residual light from the men's torch. He was confident that if he hid behind the sarcophagus base at the back of the right-hand room, he would not be seen. Freddie easily dropped down the short distance and – just in time – crept into position as the men emerged back into the same room through a tiny, low entrance.

Ay was speaking. "It is a fine, small tomb, a perfect

tribute to a small irrelevant life. I have far outgrown this place. It will now serve a greater purpose. It is ready to be used, I think." His sinister laugh echoed eerily down the tunnel.

What was Ay talking about? This must be his tomb. But if so, why all the secrecy? And what did he mean about it being ready to be used? Freddie's mind was racing again. He wanted to leave, but was petrified of making a noise. He concentrated on calming his breathing and lying as still as possible.

Userhat helped Ay back up to the first room, where they were discussing something about another entrance. Userhat was scrabbling dirt from the floor, but Freddie couldn't see properly.

"The second tunnel is behind this wall," Userhat said. "I have invented a secret mechanism to turn these two blocks of stone. It gives a small man the chance to enter the tomb unobserved. There's a confined space on the other side, and on the floor are two levers. The first will close this wall again leaving no trace of intrusion, and the second lever opens two blocks in the treasury chamber, where we were just now. That in turn gives access to the burial chamber through the low entrance. Let me show you, great Lord Ay."

Freddie peered above the rim of the sarcophagus base and through the opening to the next room. He saw Userhat pull a lever up from a shallow trench on the floor. Simultaneously, two solid stone blocks turned silently and smoothly, revealing a narrow gap, one that a small man could squeeze through reasonably easily. But even Userhat, who was painfully thin, struggled to get through. After a brief moment the two stones turned back to close the wall again.

Ay stood back and admired the brilliance of the secret entrance. All of a sudden, from the room straight ahead of Freddie, a scraping noise was heard and a pulse of stale air wafted through.

There followed the sound of stones and dirt being repacked into a hole in the ground, and then Userhat, covered in powdery dust, emerged into the burial chamber via the low gap, and then up again to rejoin Ay in the first room. He had done a round trip.

Userhat stood before Ay, who laughed again, but this time it seemed to be with admiration for the assistant architect, who filled in the lever trench, packing it down with his foot.

Why did Ay need an escape route from his own tomb? Surely he would be dead and unable to use it!

"That is not all, great Lord," said Userhat, inclining his head slightly in a bow. "A second tunnel has been created beyond the wall; a steep, narrow pipe that a lean man can climb down. So once the tomb is officially closed and sealed, it will be easy to access and no one will be any the wiser. I think I have exceeded your instructions, great Lord. I hope you are pleased with my efforts."

To Freddie, all this could only mean a robbery. Was Ay planning for someone to plunder his own treasures from his tomb after he died? It didn't make sense. Freddie was eager to try the mechanisms and find the secret pipe tunnel behind the wall. He needed to figure out what this all meant.

As he strained to hear what they were talking about, his sandal slipped slightly on the dirt floor. The men stopped and listened. Freddie held his breath, not daring to move a single muscle.

"Just a trickle of loose plaster, my Lord. I will check everything is in order." Userhat retraced his steps back through the burial chamber and into the farthest room with the second secret entrance.

"Yes, my Lord, I must have loosened some plaster near the turning blocks in here. It will be easily mended the next time I come. No one will notice until then, I can assure you."

"I hope you're right, because if this is discovered, I will deny all knowledge of these alterations to my tomb."

"Indeed, my Lord. I understand."

"How does one find the entrance to the second tunnel?"

"I will show you as we leave, my Lord, but it is cleverly disguised as a pit for rubbish and has a false wooden bottom, below which is the top of the pipe tunnel."

This reassurance seemed to seal the deal. Ay stretched out the fingers of his left hand and removed two huge rings, which he dropped into the waiting palm of the oily assistant architect who then slipped them on his own fingers.

"And why the two secret entrances?"

"Aah! If you remember, my Lord, the burial chamber will be completely inaccessible after the nominated party is interred, so access to the treasury chamber will be by the second mechanism and not through this doorway, which will be filled and sealed." He pointed at the head-high entrance to the room where Freddie was hiding.

"Who else knows about this?" asked Ay, with his face suddenly darkening in threat.

"No one. Well, no one *living*!" replied Userhat, with a snake-like smile. "The men who created this masterpiece, under my instruction, have gone forward to the next life, slightly earlier than any of them had planned. You remember the collapse of the wall at the workers' village? It was no accident. I engineered it to fall when the men were sitting on the other side, waiting for their work shift. It was a shame. It was a lovely wall... very well built."

"And the men who pushed over the wall?"

"Ah! An even sadder tale, my great Lord. A tragedy. All were lost and drowned as their boat sank on the Nile on their way to work on the ram-headed sphinxes at Karnak. There are so many crocodiles at this time of year. I never cross the river if I can help it."

Ay laughed at this news. Things really were going very well for him, it seemed. "A masterwork, Userhat. A wonder indeed."

After checking all was in place and extinguishing the torch, the two men left the chambers and made their way cautiously upwards through the dark towards the daylight. Freddie heard Userhat say, "There will be a surprise for anyone who discovers the tunnel by chance. A very terrible end awaits..." But his voice was lost in the echoes of their footsteps.

Freddie waited a few more seconds to be safe. In the dark, he made his way to where he thought the extinguished torch was on the ground. He cast around with his hand and found the handle on his third sweep. A tiny glow shone out. Freddie gently blew and the ember brightened and spread, until he had a flame back. The first thing he did was check that the men had gone, and then he returned to the first chamber to test the mechanisms for himself. He located the lever in the floor and after a hefty pull, the stones slid around as easily as he had observed before.

Freddie marvelled at the ingenuity and engineering of the secret way in and out. He lay on his front and carefully pushed the flaming torch through into the space beyond, then squeezed through and stood up. It was tight, but there was easily room for two people.

He held the torch up to see the escape pipe Userhat had talked about run off vertically at about his shoulder height. At his feet were two undisguised levers. He half pulled them both, not wanting to trap himself in this tight space. *What was the purpose of it all?*

Robbery had to be the only answer. Kha had told Freddie that tombs were often plundered, especially if people didn't like the pharaohs buried there. *But this isn't a pharaoh's tomb,* Freddie puzzled.

Freddie would have to work out what was going on. All he knew so far was that Ay planned to rob himself when he was dead, which didn't make sense.

He slid back into the tomb and covered his tracks. He memorised the layout and paced the rooms, measuring them in strides.

Five minutes later and hidden at the entrance, he blinked for a minute or so in the bright midday sun and saw to his left what had to be the pit that disguised the secret passage. It would take some digging but it would be worth it for a robber, knowing what treasures were buried down below.

Checking he was alone, he measured the pit's position by pacing between all the landmarks he could find, like prominent rocks and dried-up flood gullies that scarred the face of the hillside. Although the valley was completely deserted, once again, Freddie had the uncomfortable feeling he was not alone.

Chapter 8

Freddie's painfully hot trek saw him safely back in the royal apartments, and with Kha and Ankha still absent, he decided to cool off in the underground labyrinth below the palace.

It was easy to navigate as the channels were just wide enough for him to float in the shallow water. He could pull himself along using the walls and there was plenty of light, as the ducts ran alongside gardens. Every so often a tributary would feed a different set of rooms or ponds. Freddie mapped his progress easily by popping his head up and spotting familiar places above ground. He was having great fun relaxing in the cool waters.

Just as he was thinking of turning back, he spied the distinctive figure of Ay hurrying through a leafy courtyard, followed by Userhat. So loathsome was the assistant architect that Freddie expected to see a trail of slime where he'd been walking.

Ay disappeared to the left and Freddie could easily pick out the channel to follow underground. Feeling like James Bond, he moved under the floors and after 30 metres, emerged in Ay's courtyard garden.

Freddie's head was brilliantly camouflaged by the foliage growing around the spout that was feeding a pool of brightly coloured fish. Userhat faced away from Freddie, whilst Ay anxiously paced the marble floor, listening intently.

It was difficult for Freddie to hear everything because of the gurgle of the running water, but what he did hear chilled him. "It must be *tonight*," Ay said. "Put the invasion plans in his room while they eat." Userhat began to explain how difficult it would be to carry out Ay's wishes and what a huge personal risk he was taking. He hoped his reward would adequately reflect the danger he faced. Ay's stare silenced the thin man immediately. He moved close and said, "Put it in the fish. I'll distract her at the vital moment."

"I will try, my great Lord, but it will not be easy."

"Silence!" Ay said disdainfully. "Signal to me when it is done. Make no mistakes. Your rewards will be plentiful in the miraculous times to come. Don't fail me, or by Osiris I will finish you." He handed his lackey a roll of papyrus tied with a distinctive thin blue leather strap. Userhat nodded.

"I will not fail you, great Lord Ay," he replied, wiping the sweat from his neck before walking backwards and bowing low as he made his exit. *This was a privilege normally reserved for the pharaoh himself,* Freddie thought.

Still lying in the cooling waters, Freddie couldn't believe the success of both of his spying missions. His mind was racing with the day's revelations. He desperately needed to speak with Kha.

He watched on now as firstly Ay replenished his left hand with rings, and then walked over to a curtain. He pulled it back to reveal a shocking sight. A man, woman and two children sat huddled, gagged and bound in a strong wooden cage. They flinched under Ay's stare. He simply laughed and closed the curtain again, before leaving his quarters.

Freddie slipped away down the channel. Once back in his room, he dried himself, dressed and tried to work out what was going on.

What would be disguised by the taste of fish? What was the relevance of the tomb's hidden mechanisms? Why was Userhat taking a papyrus scroll away from Ay? And what did it contain? Who were the four people tied up in a cage in Ay's chambers?

Freddie liked it best when just he, Kha and Ankha, with maybe the tutors and the handmaids, ate their evening meal together. But tonight a feast was arranged for the conclusion of the royal visit and the imminent departure to Memphis, almost a week's journey north towards the sea.

He didn't get a chance to speak with either of them before the long process of preparing the royal couple began. Freddie was turned away from both their private rooms by Ay's guards.

In the beautifully decorated central courtyard the tables were positioned around the outside to form an open square so everyone could see the king and queen as they dined. In the centre, musicians perched on cushions, and servants knelt with wine and water on hand to fill any goblet as soon as it was empty. Tiny flames from a thousand oil lamps created a fairy-tale atmosphere now that the sky above was dark. The stars as their ceiling added to the magical setting.

Freddie looked for his place and was dismayed to find he was as far away from Kha as it was possible to get, as if his inclusion was an inconvenient afterthought.

As everyone assembled, he found himself stuck between the wife of the Hittite ambassador on one side, and the daughter of a Nubian trader on the other. They both completely ignored Freddie and talked across him as if he wasn't there.

A fanfare sounded and the royal couple entered, followed by Ay and Horemheb, Khensuhotep and Nibamon, with Dedu lolloping along faithfully behind his master and sniffing at strangers. Kha wore his magnificent striped Nemes head cloth, boasting the powerful vulture and cobra symbols. He and Ankha took their places and cast their eyes around the assembly until they saw Freddie tucked away in the corner. Kha looked angry that his friend was not closer but his attention was diverted by Ay, who indicated it was time to speak. His second speech of the day.

"I thank you for coming to bid us farewell. Tomorrow we leave for the comfort of Memphis and home. It has been a difficult time for me here, but I am grateful for the many kindnesses that you have bestowed on me. I am happy also with the work on the avenue of ram-headed sphinxes at Karnak and also my magnificent tomb, which we viewed today. Such skills show why Egypt is the greatest power in the world. I thank you all and command only one thing: that you enjoy your evening. By the great god Amun, who sleeps until the sunrise, enjoy your feast." With that he sat and a hundred plates of exotic fruits appeared and the hungry gathering started to eat.

Freddie caught Kha's eye, but his warning gesture was obscured by passing servants. Ay, who was sat next to Ankha diverted the king's attention with an introduction to an important emissary from Mittani.

And then the fish was served.

A sudden and urgent panic triggered every nerve in Freddie's being, and his heart began to pound.

He watched as huge platters of delicious-looking grilled fish were ceremoniously carried in and were placed on the tables in front of the guests. Then everyone waited for the royal couple's food to arrive.

Userhat appeared from the shadows and made eye contact with Ay. Freddie gently swung his legs clear of his chair, knowing he might have to move quickly.

Another fanfare sounded and two golden platters followed the portly figure of the royal chef. Behind him, walked the even larger figure of the pharaoh's food taster. But he was not the man who usually appeared briefly at the beginning of every meal and nodded assent to indicate the food was wholesome and safe.

He bowed and ostentatiously wiped the corners of his mouth with a cloth, indicating to the royal couple that all was well with the food. Then he walked away backwards, narrowly avoiding the loitering Dedu who was ever hopeful of scraps.

Servants placed plump portions of catfish before Kha and Ankha. All the guests' eyes were on the first royal mouthful so that they could begin.

Ay deliberately engaged Ankha in conversation, diverting her attention from Kha. Freddie knew this was the critical moment. The substitute food taster slipped into the shadows, followed immediately by Userhat. Freddie rose from his seat and moved swiftly round the outside of the tables. Everything around him seemed to be happening in slow motion: Kha, still fussing Dedu; Ay forcing Ankha's attention his way; the food taster now hurrying towards the main entrance of the palace, followed by Userhat; and finally, Kha reaching his hand out towards the fish platter before him.

Freddie dodged servants pouring wine as he tried frantically to reach Kha, but was still too far away as he tore into his fish. Freddie was not going to get there in time.

Kha raised the fish to his mouth and a hundred people did likewise, all keen to enjoy the banquet. Freddie leaped onto the table top between two elderly men and yelled, "NO! Kha, NO!" His desperate shout cut through the air. All eyes turned to the small, mousey-haired boy. Freddie leaped towards Kha, scattering servants and musicians in his wake. Several tried to stop him but Freddie was at full speed and he dodged and ducked their efforts.

With the fish just centimetres from Kha's mouth, Freddie shouted again, "NO! Kha. Stop! It's poisoned, I'm sure of it. SSSTTTOOOPPP!"

Life moved on frame by frame: Ankha began to turn towards Kha; Ay started to stand; two guards vaulted the table to intercept Freddie; and Horemheb drew his sword. Kha's expression changed from puzzlement to horror as Ay screamed the order to kill.

Freddie ducked the first sword sweep and dived to push the fish away from Kha's mouth. Goblets of wine spilled and plates of food clattered on the mosaic floor as Freddie skidded along the tabletop.

Everything clicked on in a series of sharp images as people scattered, guards jumped up and Freddie saw the look of alarm Ankha's face as Kha's loyal guard, Parennefer, raced forward to protect his king.

Dedu, thinking all his doggy prayers had been answered at once, plunged under the table to gorge on the spilled food as Kha's golden platter landed on the floor beside him. With one easy grab, the beautiful beast, with a disbelieving gleam in his eye, swallowed the entire fish from his master's plate in two large gulps.

Freddie shouted, "NO! Dedu, NO!" But it was too late.

Everyone in the room was on their feet in panic except for Ay, who sat down heavily, staring at the small boy from Albanicus who had thwarted his plans. Freddie began to call to Kha but then Horemheb's huge hand covered his mouth and held him impossibly tight.

A strange quiet descended. Then Ay rose and surveyed the room. He spoke in a measured, strong and clear voice.

"It is obvious to me that this boy, this spy, has just made an attempt on our great Pharaoh's life. This foreigner has wormed his way to the very seat of power, waiting for a chance to assassinate King Tutankhamun, chosen of the gods. We witnessed it ourselves and it is obvious to me, and I am sure to all of you, what his punishment must be."

He nodded at Horemheb who still held Freddie in his vice-like grip. The grizzly old soldier raised his sword and was about to bring it down when an anguished howl cut through the air. Dedu was frothing at the mouth, with his beautiful amber eyes rolling back in his head. He staggered from under the table, shaking violently and buckling in the throes of a terrible sickness.

Everyone had seen him gorge the fish from Kha's platter and they had all seen Freddie try to stop the king from eating it. They all knew instantly that Freddie had saved the life of the young boy king Tutankhamun.

Ay shouted at Horemheb, "What are you waiting for? Kill the spy!"

The shocked soldier looked to Kha for his verdict. In a leap of breathtaking agility, the boy king vaulted the table, pushed aside the threatening sword and fell to the floor clutching his beloved dying dog in his arms.

He screamed, "Catch the food taster! I want him here alive. I want to know who planned this. Call my physicians, NOW! Get out all of you. I hate it here. I hate this place!"

Chapter 9

All the guests were hurriedly ushered away. The royal party, with Kha carrying the dying Dedu, and Ankha supporting her sobbing husband, made for the safety of their quarters. Horemheb followed with Freddie, still tightly restrained, and on Ay's instructions with a hand still firmly over his mouth.

Once in the large day room, Dedu was attended to by the king's physicians. Kha lay at his side, stroking the faithful dog, whose tiny, shallow breaths became fewer and further between. With one final sigh the dog's eyes opened. He licked Kha's comforting hand, then his head fell back and he was still and silent.

Kha held the dog in his arms and wept with heartbreaking sobs.

Ay spoke first. "Your Majesty, our condolences about your dog Desu—"

"*Dedu!*" spat Kha, through his anger and tears.

"Dedu. Yes of course. There will be a full investigation as to how this terrible event occurred, and the guilty parties will be caught and—"

At that moment a party of guards brought in a wailing, bloodstained figure. The corpulent food taster was thrown to the ground and from behind him stepped Userhat. He glanced at Ay and bowed deeply to his king. "My gracious Lord, pharaoh of the Two Lan—"

"Not you again," moaned Horemheb. "What is it? What happened?"

"This man, this terrible man," began Userhat, "I saw him leave the feast as the food was served. I followed and caught him trying to steal a chariot. I called for the guards, but before they could help me I was attacked. I only just managed to draw my knife in time. We fought long and hard before I could overpower him. Sadly, I cut his tongue out with a move to defend myself, or you would be able to hear the villain himself tell you it was the truth." Several of Ay's soldiers glanced at each other with subtly raised eyebrows at Userhat's version of events.

The food taster lay on the floor, shaking his head and making gurgling noises, but his words were unintelligible.

"How fortunate our king is to have such loyal subjects who risk their lives in pursuit of justice," Ay said. "Remove this vermin away and finish what the loyal Userhat has started. Display his carcass in the city so all can see that the threat has been ended." With that, four soldiers dragged the food taster away.

Dedu's limp body was retrieved from Kha's grasp, wrapped in a golden cloth and taken away. Ankha comforted her husband, who now looked all the more like a frail child in a land of scheming giants. He cast his eyes around the room until he saw Freddie, still held in the iron grip of Horemheb. Kha ran to Freddie, pushing the soldier's arms away and hugging his friend in grateful thanks.

"You have saved my life again, Freddie Malone. You are my most loyal subject and you will be at my side forever. You—"

"Your Majesty!" started Ay in protest.

"Be quiet! I am speaking," roared Kha. "Freddie is the most loyal subject I have, and he's not even Egyptian. Without him I would be twice dead."

"We need to talk," whispered Freddie to Kha. "Now. Please. It's urgent. I've got a lot of things to tell you." Kha nodded, but before they got the chance, Userhat spoke again, addressing the king directly.

"Your supreme highness, I'd advise you to step away from this boy. He is in league with your enemies and plots the downfall of Egypt and your subsequent death at the hands of the invading Albanic forces, who are massing at our northwestern borders, according to a scout who arrived this afternoon. All this was contained in a papyrus that a messenger brought for your loyal viziers to act upon. Mysteriously, the scout disappeared, and for many hours could not be found. He was last seen handing the papyrus to Horemheb's assistant Minnakht, who reports it stolen from his rooms. This boy" – he indicated Freddie – "was seen loitering near his chamber a short while later."

"That's all lies!" cried out Freddie. All eyes turned to him but Userhat continued.

"And sadly, I have to report that the body of the messenger was found just now hidden in undergrowth in the palace gardens."

Kha ran at Userhat and unleashed a vicious sweep of his arm across the obnoxious man's face.

"Are you mad? I am the king. This is my most loyal friend. He is not capable of such treachery. Since when did an assistant architect gain such knowledge of these mighty affairs? You have been taught to say all this by someone else. And before you die, you will tell me who that is."

"But my Lord," cried Userhat, visibly shaken, and wiping blood from his cut lip, "your so-called loyal friend has the papyrus. Search his room if you don't believe me. He must be hiding it there, if he hasn't destroyed it already. Kill me if you don't find it in his possession."

Kha limped towards Freddie's room. He threw

clothes and sandals around looking for a papyrus he knew was not there.

Except it was.

There, amongst an untidy pile of clothes was the rolled papyrus with the distinctive blue tie. No doubt Userhat had hidden it there while the guests had assembled for the feast. Kha looked shocked and Ankha gasped.

Freddie cried, "No, Kha! It's been planted here. I promise."

Ay strode forward with a condescending smile on his face. "My Lord, do you believe me now? Surely not even your ill-advised friendship with this dangerous spy can blind you to the fact that he has hidden the proof that his country Albanicus is about to invade, seize the kingdom and kill you into the bargain."

Freddie protested. "It's not true! Believe me!"

Kha gently put his hand on Freddie's arm and nodded reassuringly, silencing his protests. Ankha unrolled the papyrus, studying it carefully as Ay continued.

"Our scouts tell me how dangerous this mighty nation Albanicus has become, my Lord. It is full of bloodthirsty non-believers who worship the darkness and who would seek our destruction." Freddie wondered at Ay's ability to lie and scheme. "A true politician!" Uncle Patrick would have said.

Ankha looked up from the scroll and smiled at her husband as she said in a hushed tone, "There is something very familiar in the style of this message – a very distinct and familiar hand, one I have seen often. It looks to me as though the vizier Ay has penned this warning, and not an army commander on our country's border. I would know his hand anywhere. After all, we see it three times a day."

Ankha shared a look of understanding with Kha, who nodded and looked from Ay to Freddie.

"It seems we have two stories. One, a well-rehearsed and complicated version of events told by people I wouldn't want to be in a room alone with – and a second, simply demonstrated by the actions of a loyal and trusted friend, who has saved my life twice and who has been unable to voice his story because he has been forcibly silenced. Now he will tell me everything he knows and at first light you will gather to hear it too. Then I will decide who will live and who will pay for their lies."

Ay spoke angrily. "But why wait? Let's hear from him now. If we wait until morning he has time to invent an excuse, or worse, he could escape, or he could kill you as you sleep."

"Be silent," said Kha. "We have heard so much more from you than anyone should ever have to. I will not be murdered in my sleep by this boy. Someone else may well try, for I am surrounded by treachery. I sleep always with one eye open, ready for an attack. Ready for a treasonous puppet to slit my throat for gold."

Kha turned to Userhat. "What have you been promised, assistant architect? A position in Ay's palace when he becomes pharaoh? A villa with land? A burial tomb in the sacred valleys? All of these, I shouldn't wonder. Until this boy arrived less than two moons ago, I would never have spoken like this, but he has given me the courage to see people for what they really are, to look them in the eyes and call them liars. There are many in this room whom, come the morning, I will look in the eye and call 'liar'. And Freddie will not be one of them.

"Go now," he continued, "All of you except my trusted wife Ankhesenamun and my loyal friend. I will hear his story, and in the morning you will hear my decision. We will depart for Memphis as soon as possible and we will leave behind this nest of snakes. We will return to the land of pyramids and the broad river, and we will never return to this terrible place, except when the twelve stages of night see me safely face-to-face with Osiris.

"Parennefer and my loyal guards will watch our doors tonight and will deny entry to anyone until first light," Kha continued, looking directly at Ay and waving everyone away.

The three intrepid teenagers watched everyone leave, as Parennefer stationed double guards at all the doors. Freddie even asked for two to be placed by the water inlet to thwart anyone who might try to use his stealthy way of navigating the palace.

When everyone was gone, the three sank down on the couches and looked at each other with a mixture of wonder, sadness, and fierce determination.

They had a lot of talking to do before morning.

Chapter 10

"What happened? How did you escape the Whizzer guy?"

"Whizzer? You mean vizier!"

"Same thing," smiled a spellbound Connor.

Freddie sat back and laughed. He'd been talking for an hour, with Connor hanging on his every word. But he needed a rest and refreshment, which arrived courtesy of Mrs M.

"It's lovely to see you boys gassin', y'know," she said. "Not a phone or a tablet in sight." She almost skipped back inside the house where the unmistakable smell of muffins was wafting out from the kitchen.

Freddie quietly continued. "By now, we were all starving. We had to get the guards to bring some safe food from the tables. But no fish – no way!"

At that moment, as Freddie was about to launch back into his adventure, a splintering of wood, followed by a crash, split the air. It came from next door. Both Freddie and Connor leaped on to the midway rail of the fence. Well, Freddie leaped up and Connor managed to step up at the third attempt. They peered over.

There, on the ground, lying amidst what remained of a shattered garden chair, was Ruby. She had obviously been listening and had climbed on the old rotten furniture the Wilton's had left behind when they moved.

Freddie wanted to laugh but a terrible thought struck him. He swallowed hard and felt a little sick. Someone else had heard everything he had reported to Connor.

Ruby got up quickly, smoothed her clothes down and brushed the crazy blue wavy tress out of her eyes. It was the first time Freddie had seen her look flustered.

"What's wrong with you two? Never seen anyone chop firewood before?"

You had to hand it to Ruby, she was quick. She then easily scaled the flat fence her side, perching briefly on top before jumping effortlessly down on to Freddie's patio. She turned and helped Connor descend from the midway bar as he tried to untangle his jumper, which was snagged on a splinter of rough wood.

Ruby pulled a face at them both.

"You don't half go on," she said and shook her head in wonder. "I thought you were reading a book out loud to Whatshisname here, but you just went on and on. I've never heard anything like it. Is it for homework or something? I bet I could make up stuff like that, easy as anything." She paused for breath.

"Yes it's homework, English homework... stuff!" Freddie blurted. "And this is not 'Whatshisname'. He's called Con—"

"AAH! Stuff! So this is the 'stuff' you were on about. Brilliant, I can help you with 'stuff', no probs."

"Thanks, but I'm finished now, the story. The 'stuff' is all done."

"So you're just going to let it all stop there? You can't do that. How about if he escapes during the night? And what about the weird Eye bloke? People will want to know the end. I'll finish it if you want."

Freddie looked aghast at Connor. Ruby had heard everything. How could they get out of this one?

Connor's stomach felt tight. The map. Had she heard all about the map too?

"Err... when did you start listening to err... the *stuff*?"

"Since you came out here, I think," she answered. "Everything, the tombs, the secret passage, the pipe tunnel, the underground waterways, the poisoned fish, dead Dedu, *everything*! You must be top of the class at English because that was very convincing buddy. You had me believing you were there!"

Freddie held his hands out by his sides. "What can I say? I just *lurve* Egypt. I get carried away."

Ruby nodded. "Cool," she replied.

Both boys began to breathe more easily.

Talk about football, she obviously likes it, just keep talking about that and she'll forget all about Egypt, Connor thought to himself. But as he opened his mouth to ask her what team she supported, Ruby spoke first.

"So what's all that about the map on your wall?"

Connor stared at Freddie, thinking he was about to have a heart attack. Freddie looked pale. He took a very deep breath and asked her to sit down.

Half an hour later they sat back exhausted – and surprisingly unburdened. It felt good to be able to tell someone else about their adventures so far. All about the map, the mountains, Mingma and Mindhu, and the amazing powers of the poem 'If—'.

Ruby sat back as well. "So that's what you two

randoms mean by 'stuff'? I'd better see this map of yours before I make my mind up about you, buddy."

A short while later, after a confusing episode in the kitchen introducing Ruby to Mrs M and eating, in Connor's case, a record three muffins in five minutes, the three of them found themselves in front of the wondrous world map, complete and magnificent again on Freddie's bedroom wall.

The colours appeared more vibrant than usual, as if it had preened itself and was showing off. Ruby studied it from every angle, examined the wall behind it, then tried to spot Neptune moving, which he didn't. She rubbed her finger over Niagara Falls to see if it was wet. Nothing. There was no sign of any disturbance, no water, no roaring sphinx.

After a lengthy pause, she turned to them both, burst out laughing and elbowed Connor painfully in the side of his stomach. "You two desperados are good, I'll give you that. That story was amazing. Wowzer!" She stood back from the map again, inclining her head in thought. "But I don't believe a word of it. I'm going to have to see you disappear through the wall myself to swallow all that. And now you've been to Egypt as well. Are you mad? If you only got back at 3 am, how come there's no sign of damage? My bedroom's the other side of this map, so your vortex thingammy would go straight through my room if you dived through here. Well, I can tell you there's no time tunnel in our house."

Freddie and Connor looked at each other. This was exactly the result they wanted but weren't expecting. They shared a miniscule smile, but Freddie really wanted to do a double fist pump. Result!

"You two are barking mad. Brilliant, but barking," giggled Ruby with a huge generous smile. "I don't believe a word of it. But at least you're not boring. A couple of stories like that a week will keep me going, I can tell you. Let's finish the Egypt one – what's happening there, then?"

Connor was looking down at the garden.

"Your mum's at the fence. She wants something," he blurted, feeling the need to fall to his knees in relief. Ruby threw up the sash window and shouted down excitedly, "I'm up here with my friends, Mum. They're actually great, not dead boring and sad like I said yesterday."

Freddie and Connor raised their eyebrows at each other. Freddie laughed. It felt like life in Normandy Avenue was never going to be the same again, and from the look on Connor's face, his friend felt the same. Ruby was called in to help with the twins' tea.

"You can come with us in the morning to the oak, if you like," Freddie heard himself say.

Ruby pulled a face.

"Might do," she quietly pondered. "So then, I've got to look out for a bunch of idiots in tracksuits: a tall, mean-looking, sporty guy with eyes like blue lasers, a little scruffy one, and a few in between?"

Connor nodded. "Exactly, that's them!"

Ruby turned to go but suddenly swung back around and pointed at Freddie.

"Hey, bud, don't you come bursting through my bedroom wall tonight, coz I'll borrow Archie's baseball bat and give you a right twang if you do."

Freddie nodded.

"Don't worry, I won't. Come round here about 9:30 in the morning and I'll show you the way to the oak. And please don't tell anyone about the Egypt thing, all right? It's just between us, OK?"

"Of course I won't. I'm not stupid!"

And with that, she was gone.

Connor collapsed on the bed, exhausted. Freddie sank to his chair. What had just happened? Someone else knew about the map and, to make matters worse, it was someone new and potentially crazy. At least Ruby thought the adventures were all invented.

"She thinks you're an ace storyteller, and that we're winding her up," Connor stated, staring at the ceiling. "What a result!"

"Yes," Freddie replied cautiously. "Shall I just

not be here at 9:30?"

"No! I mean, she thinks we're idiots who make stuff up. She may as well hear the rest."

Freddie grinned. "You fancy her, don't you?"

Connor went bright red. "Nope. No, *deffo* not!" He shook his head as he sat up.

Freddie nodded. "Because I think even *you* would be biting off more than you could chew with Ruby."

"Don't know what you mean," Connor said defensively. "Anyway, you've got to carry on with the story. But seriously, Freddie, please promise me one thing," he added earnestly. "Promise me that Ruby won't be in charge. And promise me I get to go on the next adventure – and if Ruby tries to muscle in, you've got to say, 'It's Connor's turn next.' Promise me, Freddie, *please*."

Freddie was taken aback by his friend's sudden anxiety.

"Don't worry, mate, I promise. She thinks we're crackers, so what are we worried about? We've just got to stop her talking at school."

Both boys stared at the map.

"Loose cannon," said Freddie. "She's a loose cannon, that's what Dad would say."

"Home time, Connor, darlin'," called Mrs M, from below. As the boys went downstairs, in came Finnegan and Kathleen. Mr Malone had picked them up on his way home from work. Connor made a super-fast exit as Finnegan started swearing loudly, struggling to get his arms out of his old overcoat.

As Freddie helped the old man, Finnegan whispered quietly, "Are you looking after that map, boy? It's a precious thing and needs great care and attention... I should imagine."

Freddie nodded.

"Tea's ready," called Mr M from the kitchen.

"What is it?" retorted Finnegan, at his normal volume.

"Stew, boys!"

"Huh! Stew again!" complained Finnegan, "I've had enough stew to last ten lifetimes," and he shuffled grumpily into the noisy kitchen.

Connor's mind raced as he wandered in the general direction of his house. As amazing as Freddie's Egyptian tale was, his main worry and fascination was centred entirely on Ruby. He was petrified about the wonderful world he shared with Freddie being opened up and spoiled by new people. People who didn't fully understand everything, or who wanted to sabotage things, or make fun of them.

He was also petrified of Ruby. She was strong, funny, persuasive, funny, clever and funny. Very funny! And Connor thought she was gorgeous as well. Freddie was right about that. So she was magnetic and dangerous in equal measure.

He zigzagged home through the dusky autumn streets to a silent welcome, all except a TV game show blaring at near-Finnegan volume. In four microwave minutes his tea was piping hot, and he spent an evening in front of the television with his mum, dad and brother Carl, watching programmes about vets, police chases and people with tattoos of celebrities on their bodies – at this low point, Connor went to bed.

He looked up 'Egyptian Kings' on his phone and up popped the names and dates of all the pharaohs. It showed the families and dynasties to which each one belonged.

He scrolled down. Suddenly, there it was:

18th Dynasty of the New Kingdom. Tutankhamun [previously called Tutankhaten] 1333 BC–1323 BC [approx.], married to Queen Ankhesenamun. Two children who died in infancy.

A shudder coursed through Connor as he looked at the dates. Freddie was in Egypt in 1328 BC, about halfway through Kha's ten-year reign, which meant he had five years left to rule and would be dead by the time he was 18 or 19 years old.

Then a second, even stronger, shudder rocked

Connor as he saw the name of the pharaoh that succeeded Kha. The name 'Ay' leaped out at him.

"Nnnnoooo!" he whispered. Then he read the name of Ay's wife. 'Ankhesenamun'.

"Oh no! Poor Kha. Poor Ankha. What a nightmare." He scribbled all this down on a piece of paper, and as he drifted off to sleep he thought of the young royal couple, their devotion and fierce loyalty to Freddie, which was nearly as strong as his own.

What would the rest of Freddie's tale reveal in the morning? What would Ruby make of it all? He couldn't wait to find out.

Chapter 11

As Connor approached the great oak tree, he was shocked to find Freddie and Ruby already in place. Not only that, they were studying a notebook and talking excitedly. What was even worse, Ruby was perched in Connor's usual place. She didn't pause for breath as Connor clumsily hauled himself up through the lower branches, and she didn't acknowledge his arrival, so involved was she in the lecture she was giving to Freddie on ancient Egypt.

Freddie smiled and nodded at Connor, then fist-bumped his friend as he edged past, climbing to a vacant higher branch. It wasn't nearly as comfy as his usual spot, which Ruby had now made her own.

"He had two kids with Ankha, but they both died young. And she – get this, buddy – she only went and married the 'Ay' man. What's that all about? You said she hated him. You'll have to change that bit in the story when you write it down. What else...? Morning, Conman!" Ruby finally acknowledged Connor's arrival.

Connor nodded with a weak smile.

"Oh! Yeah, Kha ruled for about ten years and no one knows how he died, so you can make that bit up when you come to it."

She finally drew breath. Freddie smiled and turned to Connor.

"Ruby was just suggesting ways to finish the story, and I said I had to wait until you came so you didn't miss anything."

"Thanks." Connor smiled more genuinely this time. "I found out all that stuff as well—"

"So carry on, Freddie," interrupted Ruby.

Connor felt snubbed and looked to his best friend for support. But rather than give Freddie the problem of 'sulky best friend' to worry about on top of everything else – and because he was eager to hear how things developed – Connor kept quiet.

"All right, all right," laughed Freddie, sharing a look of pretend horror with Connor. "There's no rush, we've got all—"

"I'll finish it if you can't," Ruby piped up.

"No!" said Connor forcefully, then more quietly, "I mean no, sorry, Ruby. It's Freddie's story, he has to tell it. You can tell the next one if you want."

"All right then. Good idea, Conman. I like the way you're thinking, buddy. I'm gonna make one up about space and planets and killer creatures. It'll be brill, you just wait."

And so, as Ruby and Connor made themselves as comfortable as is possible when perched on worn branches five metres up a huge oak tree, Freddie continued his saga.

The loyal Parennefer returned with plenty of food as Kha confided in Freddie.

"I need your help now more than ever. Someone is trying to finish my rule over Egypt, though why I do not know."

"Greed and power," suggested Parennefer.

"Yes, you're probably right. Why else do men plot and kill? So please be vigilant, not only tonight, but on our long journey home to Memphis. We begin tomorrow. I need you both close by me at all times and ever watchful for an attack on either me, or my glorious queen."

"What about Freddie?" asked Ankha with concern. "I think he's in real danger, we must protect him as well."

"First, let us hear what Freddie has learned about our enemies, then we will make up our minds. We will have a plan long before daylight."

Freddie whispered his concerns about the suspicious guard Rudjek, and Parennefer sent the squat man on a spurious mission across the river to Karnak where he'd be gone for hours. The rest of the guards were ever-present in the shadows, alert to any possibility of attack.

Freddie explained about the second tomb, the magical stone-turning mechanisms, the gift of the rings, and Userhat taking the scroll from Ay. Then he described how he had spied on the vizier from the water system and heard that something was to be put into the fish. None of them could make sense of it all, other than to believe that it was a plot by Ay to take the throne. It was not a surprise to Kha, as the cruel vizier behaved as if he were pharaoh anyway.

"I'm so sorry about Dedu," Freddie said. "If only I hadn't knocked your plate to the floor, he would still be alive now."

"But you would be dead," said Ankha emphatically. "That brute Horemheb would have killed you and then where would we be? We need you alive to watch over us. I am so frightened that in the morning Ay will just take you away and dispose of you, like others who have grown close to us over the years."

"We must hide you," said Kha.

"But where? We will be sailing north on the great river," Ankha replied.

"Don't worry. I'll follow you on the journey," said

Freddie, with sudden clarity. "Kha, how many boats and people travel with you?"

"At least twenty large barques on the river, some pulling supply barges and troop carriers. On each riverbank, five hundred soldiers keep pace with our progress to stop an attack from land."

Ankha took over. "We stop at dusk and moor in safety, with all the boats gathered round to protect us."

"Well, I must get on to one of your supply barges and hide myself. I'll keep a watchful eye out and warn you if I discover anything. Now, how will I do that?"

Ankha smiled triumphantly. "All Egyptians are protected by their scarab. The beetle is our guardian, not only in this life, but also in death. Kha has a special scarab that we will entrust to you. If you find out his life is in danger, you must somehow show us the sign of the scarab, or even better, show us the scarab itself, so we know we have to meet you to talk."

"That's great, but how will we meet, and when?" asked Freddie, loving the idea of the scarab.

"I know!" said Kha excitedly. "Just before the watch changes in the late evening, before Ay's night guard takes over, they get very sloppy. They think of nothing but food and sleep, so they miss many things. *Then* is the time to meet, but *where* is a different matter."

Freddie smiled. "By the tallest thing we can all see. Could be a tree, a statue, a temple. How about that?"

"Yes, but not a tree," said Kha. "It will be difficult to tell which is the tallest. So meet by the biggest man-made object that we can see. We must have disguises, Ankha. Get Kyky to make sure we have clothes that we can use to fool Ay's soldiers."

"But, my darling king and husband, everyone will know it is you by the way that you walk. It is one thing to disguise you as a priest in a chariot and fool farmers you've never met, but you'll be trying to get past people who've known you all your life."

"You could distract them, though," said Freddie to Kha. "Make a fuss and get people running around – say you need a physician or something – so while they're busy with that, Ankha can sneak out in disguise and come and meet me."

"I don't like leaving Kha alone," said Ankha.

"I can't think of another way, though," pondered Freddie.

"Freddie is right," said Kha decisively. "And you will hurry back with the news, so we can work out what to do."

Kha left the room for a short moment. When he returned he opened his cupped hands.

"Here is the scarab."

Freddie took the treasure in his own palms and cradled the beautiful turquoise scarab beetle charm. It was about three centimetres long, and half as wide, and was carved in three layers with rounded corners.

It was incredibly precious. Ankha blessed it with a wish that it would protect Freddie and return him safely to them. Freddie smiled and threaded it securely onto the string about his neck, next to Mindhu's coiled black hair – a memento from his first adventure.

From the shadows the giant Parennefer emerged. He apologised for interrupting and said, "My great king. We have ears in the palace, we can hear what is happening. I sent four men to listen to what Ay has planned for the morning. One has returned saying Ay has found Freddie's parents and had them imprisoned, ready to confess that their son is a spy. They will say so at dawn, and he will be executed immediately, no matter what you say, great son of Amun."

"Can they have found your parents?" Kha asked.

Not only was it impossible that these people were Freddie's parents, it was also impossible for him to tell Kha and Ankha that.

Parennefer intervened. "I cannot believe it, they have a darker skin than Freddie and are obviously from a country nearby us, from Takhsy or Negeb. They speak no Albanicus and protest their innocence. I believe they are nothing to do with Freddie, your majesty. But they will be forced to confess it, as Ay has their children captive too.

"It's the people I saw caged in his room."

"This is typical of Ay," said Ankha darkly.

"They aren't my parents," Freddie told her. "How

can we help them?"

"We will do all we can to release them. Parennefer and the guards will try, but it is hard. My loyal troops number so few against Ay's and Horemheb's army."

"If it is your will, great king, it will be my duty, but Freddie must leave. His presence here endangers your highness. Ay hates Freddie because he has saved your life."

"Twice," said Kha.

"Twice, indeed, great king. Now *we* must ensure you stay safe. I shall recruit more men loyal and devoted to you to continue that task."

Freddie spoke in his most determined voice. "Remember the plan. I won't be far away. I shall watch and find answers to these mysteries and I will get proof of Ay's plots against you."

"We will look after the king now, but you must go or you will be killed," said Parennefer, before disappearing into the shadows again to give orders.

The three stood silently, then, attempting a smile, Freddie said, "Don't worry. Between us, we'll protect you and keep you safe. I will use the scarab if I have anything to tell you." Then Freddie said emphatically, "This time, these days I've spent with you have been the greatest privilege a person could have. Thank you for everything."

Freddie nodded in reverence to Kha and Ankha. They said goodbye to each other and separated with tears in their eyes. The royal couple didn't seem to have any words, faced with the dreadful reality that they would be alone again. Alone against Ay.

Freddie gathered a change of clothes and made for the water system. Kha waved the guards aside to let Freddie in. Half submerged, he turned and gave as brave a smile as he could muster.

Ankha enshrouded her husband in a comforting hug and Freddie slipped fully into the dark, cool water and away.

Chapter 12

Freddie had moved as fast as possible in his wet clothes to the place where he had hidden his rucksack, and then gone on up to his lookout point. Now, many hours after his escape, he lay warming himself on the rock, having written his notes down: tomb dimensions, language, names, everything. He returned the book to the safety of its lunchbox container.

Just after dawn, thirty chariots and dozens of Ay's cavalry sped away from the palace, obviously searching for Freddie. Some headed into the distance but most were scouring the immediate area. Freddie watched their efforts but felt safe.

After two or three hours most had returned to the palace. Several teams had skirted the arena in front of Freddie, searching the undergrowth. But in the snippets Freddie picked out, their voices betrayed the fact that no one had a clue where he'd gone or how he'd escaped.

By mid-morning, as the sun became unbearably hot, Freddie saw signs of movement from the palace. The royal party started out. The dust thrown up suggested half of Egypt was with them. When they turned right opposite the temple of Hatshepsut, Freddie knew they were all heading for the landing stages opposite Luxor.

Glad to be on the move, he cut through to the riverbank and then turned north, where he could see a large cluster of boats assembled. He wrapped his headscarf so only his eyes and nose were visible, for two very good reasons. One, to protect his head from the sun, and two, to disguise himself from the hundreds of soldiers scanning the crowds.

Many troops busied themselves transferring stores and equipment to the supply barges, which were attached behind the barques by thick hemp ropes. There was so much activity by the jetties that Freddie turned inland a couple of hundred metres to find a spot where he could observe and plan. *How was he going to get on a boat with all these people about?*

Almost immediately, Freddie saw a four-wheeled prison cage rattle past with the slumped figures of two adults and two children lying against the wooden poles that held them captive. Their haunted, pleading eyes searched for help.

Hundreds of people were now gathering to watch

the grand spectacle of a passing pharaoh. Crowds, two or three deep, lined this last part of the road to the dock and as soon as Freddie had wormed his way to the front, he saw the golden chariot of his friend fast approaching, followed by Ankha and Ay close behind.

The excited citizens began to cheer and Kha generously waved back. As the chariot neared Freddie, he lowered his scarf and smiled broadly at Kha, whose eyes lit up at seeing his friend. Reassured by his presence, Kha allowed his head to turn, prolonging the contact. Freddie nodded, raised his disguise again and shrank back into the crowd.

Ay scanned the sea of faces in the direction Kha was looking, and his black eyes locked on to the disappearing shape of Freddie. He brought his chariot to an abrupt stop and screamed at his guards as Freddie darted towards the water's edge.

Ay's soldiers brutally searched the throng, pushing and shoving anyone aside who held them up. Ay drove on to the river, leaving the chaotic search in his wake. Parennefer and the loyal guard had already got Kha aboard and they now helped the queen safely onto the royal barque.

Looking back over his shoulder as he pushed through the crowd, Freddie suddenly bumped into Rudjek, the squat soldier about whom he'd had his suspicions. The soldier blinked in amazement and Freddie darted under his attempted tackle. Rudjek raised the alarm, but in the confusion Freddie was able to use people as a shield. He flitted in and out of the swirling bodies to put off the advancing soldiers.

The next moment, Freddie was by the riverbank and dozens of armed men were bearing down on him. He had no choice, so he did the only thing he could and jumped into the water, swimming to the far side of the first boat and out of direct line of sight.

Soon, he was two or three boats away from shore. He couldn't believe his luck – no one seemed to be following him. The boats appeared to be empty of people and just packed with stores, but it was difficult for Freddie to see up that high. Treading water for a moment, he put the rucksack he'd concealed under his robes, properly on his back and found progress much quicker. He was well screened by the boats, but he knew the soldiers would search until they found him.

It was all going wrong. Freddie scanned the broad river and quickly discounted the possibility of swimming all the way across. From over his right shoulder, he saw what at first looked like drifting tree trunks floating down river. Suddenly one of the tree trunks flipped in the water. It wasn't a tree trunk at all. It was a crocodile. A lethal, fully grown Nile crocodile, and it was heading straight for Freddie! He tried to scream, but just took a huge gulp of water, as more crocodiles became interested in the thrashing body in the water. Freddie pulled himself alongside the nearest boat and fumbled for a dangling rope that was just out of reach. As the crocodiles closed in, he leaped with a superhuman surge out of the water and clung to the rope, hauling himself up onto the deck of the supply barge with all the power his straining muscles could give. He turned in time to see frustrated crocs leaping up and snapping their huge jaws.

The thrashing in the water continued as a boiling knot of frustrated crocodiles searched for the prey they'd been so sure of. Shouts from the searching soldiers now filled Freddie's ears and he lifted a cooling protective cloth from a pile of stores and wormed his way into a stack of large, wooden chests, dislodging one, which toppled, smashed open and spilled huge chunks of meat over Freddie and into the water. Freddie's tunic was instantly bloodied by the spillage and an idea quickly shot through his brain. He wrapped the remaining meat in his blood-covered tunic and threw it into the water where it was shredded by angry jaws before it touched the surface. Then he replaced the wooden chest lid and hid safely amongst the others.

The crocs were still eating the meat and shredding the tunic when the first soldiers boarded the boat and looked over. Several reeled in disgust at the sight of what they thought was a small boy from Albanicus being chewed.

Then Ay himself strode to the boat's edge and if his smile was anything to go by, he seemed extremely happy the crocs had had their lunch. Freddie held his breath. He was well concealed but the soldiers didn't leave. It looked like Ay wanted to make absolutely sure his adversary was well and truly finished. The twisting knot of crocs continued to snap and fight over the last spoils, and their bloodied snouts and the red water around them at last seemed to convince them all that the boy was dead.

The evil vizier stepped onto the next barge and turned one last time. He grinned at his enemy's demise. It was a chilling moment and Freddie vowed to have some revenge on this terrible man.

Ahead of him Freddie could see the royal barque surrounded by boats full of Horemheb's soldiers. Suddenly Kha and Ankha appeared on deck, followed by the gloating figure of Ay, who had obviously just imparted the news of Freddie's end. His friends held each other tightly. Ay departed and when he was out of sight, Kha collapsed against Ankha and buried his face in her shoulder while she stroked his hair. She too was crying as she comforted her husband and gazed out at the river and the well-fed crocodiles that were now swimming away.

Freddie wished he could tell them he was safe, but that would have to wait as orders were given and the flotilla formed three lines. With a lengthy fanfare, the awkward formation drifted away from the bank to the faster-flowing water mid-stream. The pace picked up quickly and Freddie marvelled once more, as the huge temple of Karnak dominated the eastern bank. What a miracle of architecture. What an incredible achievement. What a sight!

He saw the banks of the Nile crowded with people watching and waving their pharaoh away downstream. The royal barque was shimmering in the intense heat, the golden trappings reflecting sunlight almost like a mirrorball as it made its glittering progress north, to Memphis.

Chapter 13

Freddie's luck seemed to have changed. As he cautiously left his hiding place, he could see there was just an elderly sailor, with skin like an old fashioned football, under an awning near the bow. Only once did he tour the vessel to inspect that all was well, giving Freddie time to construct a permanent hiding place. By moving the large wooden crates slightly he gave himself more room. There were huge nets with fruit of all kinds, some large jars and boxes of hard, coarse-grained bread. Food for an army on the move.

A little after dark, as the last of the boats clustered together on a tranquil bend in the river, he left his hiding place and made straight for the bread. Retrieving enough for a couple of days, he then took a leather water carrier and an earthenware jug back to his hideout. He hungrily devoured two chunks of the bread and to his delight found the jug contained some delicious small fish in olive oil. With his rucksack as a pillow he was asleep in no time.

Freddie awoke in the dark, hearing hushed voices to his right. He peered out and saw that another barque had come alongside whilst he'd slept. It was a grand boat, not quite as splendid as Kha's, but still magnificent. It appeared deserted except for the whispers coming from the one room on deck 20 metres away from Freddie.

He needed to investigate. After making sure the old leathery sailor was asleep, he left his hiding place.

There were lighted torches at the front and back of all the occupied vessels and as a result the night watch were easy to pick out. Freddie crawled and slithered along the rough wooden deck closer to the voices. He took it very slowly as he didn't want to make any more mistakes.

He got as close as he could but was disappointed to hear only chit-chat about food. Freddie was about to return to the safety of his hideout, when a torch made its way towards the voices. It was Ay! He entered the room and took the two inhabitants by surprise. A clang of metal rang out as one of the men jumped up.

"Be quiet, you dog!" Ay whispered fiercely. "Do you want Osiris himself to hear you? Who is this idiot?"

"Tuta, great Lord Ay," replied Userhat. "He is Tuta, the prisoner I recommended you release who will perform the great task and complete your destiny."

"Ah, yes," replied Ay. "Let's hope when his work finally comes, he doesn't drop the knife." He then quietly laughed at his own joke. And the unmistakable whinnying laugh of Userhat joined him.

"At least the boy is dead. That much we know. With him out of the way, your path is that much easier. He doesn't even have a dog to bark a warning now. It should be an easy job for a man of your vast experience, Tuta. I hear you are no stranger to this line of work."

"I will enjoy it, great lord. It is the one thing in life that I am good at."

"Not so good – you were caught the last time you tried," Ay smirked.

"That was an unfortunate mistake…"

"Yes, yes. I'm sure you will not fail me. After all, the consequences of doing so are too harsh to contemplate." He let Tuta absorb this, then said, "So we dock at Giza in four nights' time. There will be a ceremony in the temple of the sphinx at sunrise the next day, then a feast that night in the shadow of Khufu's Great Pyramid. You will be led to the king's tent by Rudjek, where you will wait in the darkness. After Tutankhamun's return from the feast, wait until he sleeps, then strike. If he makes a sound you will be caught. If you are silent, you will escape, as Rudjek will be watching and can conceal you as you leave. If Ankhesenamun is there, you are not to harm a hair on her head. I have other plans for her. If any harm comes to her, your death will last a thousand days and your family will follow. Do you understand?"

"Yes, great lord, I would expect nothing less," replied the slow, deep, ponderous voice of the assassin.

"Good, then we all agree. You have one task between now and then, and that is to rid me of the boy's family," he laughed. "Or his acquired relations. They were taken from a caravan of refugees fleeing the war in Retjenu and have outlasted their usefulness. Speed them on their way to the next life without anyone knowing. If you fail in this first task, you will not live long enough to perform your second."

Freddie's mind was racing. How could he release the poor captives before Tuta got to them?

"Rudjek has been allotted the same task, so it is a race between you as to who will receive the prize. In two night's' time the job will be easier. We will moor opposite the old deserted palace of Akhenaten, and the ceremony to remember the boy's mad father will preoccupy most people. You should have an easier chance of success."

"Yes, great lord. Userhat has already briefed me on that."

"You mean *my Lord* Userhat," came the slimy voice of the assistant architect. Ay laughed again, making no attempt to disguise his loathing.

"My, my, Userhat! How fast you ascend. You will be

queuing for my job as vizier once my own promotion is secure, I think." Ay fixed the assistant architect with a withering stare and Userhat laughed cautiously.

"And you, Tuta, will also find plenty of future tasks and rewards if you perform these jobs well. I never forget people who help me. And so we all march forward in the glory of the god Amun, whose representative on earth I am about to become." And with that, he slipped silently away into the night, crossing from boat to boat until his torch was indistinguishable from the hundred or so others.

Freddie had enough information to call a meeting with Kha and Ankha, but they were not in any great danger until they reached Giza. Until then, they would be very carefully guarded. Freddie's priority was to release his pretend family, and as he drifted off back to sleep in his hideout, he pondered how best he could do it.

He was awoken by the gentle movement of the barge as they sailed downstream. He had missed the start of the day's voyage but the sun was still fairly low so it wasn't long after dawn. He carefully poked his head out between two boxes and looked over the side of the barge. He was on the right-hand side of the boat staring at the east bank of the Nile floating past. Life seemed to continue happily for most Egyptians. They stopped what they were doing and either waved or flung themselves prostrate into the dirt as a mark of respect to the passing golden pharaoh. *It must have been quite a sight*, thought Freddie. Occasionally, clouds of dust on shore signalled the ever-present troops that kept pace with the flotilla in their chariots. Freddie couldn't help wondering whose side they would serve in a fight between Ay and Tutankhamun.

Behind Freddie's boat sailed Userhat and Tuta's barque. He spent the rest of the morning trying to catch a glimpse of the assassin. In his mind's eye, he built an ogre of immense proportions, but when the reality appeared it was almost a disappointment. A man the same size as Userhat emerged near midday and lowered clothes on a rope into the water and then washed them on deck. When he stood next to the assistant architect, they could have been brothers. *Perhaps they were*, Freddie thought. It would make sense.

Freddie ventured out of his hiding place only to replenish his dwindling bread and water stocks. He had uncovered yet another attempt on his friend's life. It was up to Freddie to stop it. But he had one more job before that. And it would not only be a race against time, but a race against two hardened killers.

Chapter 14

On the afternoon of the third day, the flotilla sheltered between a long island in the Nile and its eastern bank to the north of Ahketaten. From there it was easy access to the imposing palace, where Kha and the bulk of the floating population would spend a more comfortable night ashore. This was Kha's father's spectacular creation. Kha had explained to Freddie how unhappy he had been there with the very difficult Akhenaten, who was embarrassed his son was not a perfect physical specimen.

Freddie watched the royal party land, flanked by the ever faithful Parennefer, and move across some lush farmland to the palace, which was glowing in the glorious sunset. Freddie scanned the boats to see if he could locate the cage holding the prisoners. It took a while but eventually he spotted it, hard up against the island about 300 metres away.

Tuta was sitting on the deck of Userhat's barque, waiting for darkness and whittling wood with a lethal-looking long, thin knife. The thought suddenly struck Freddie that he would need something to cut the rope on the cage, as the multi-tool was in Connor's rucksack. He searched the old sailor's scattered possessions and carefully sheathed a small knife in his belt. If he left now, he would certainly be ahead of Tuta but not necessarily Rudjek, who also had the same mission.

Freddie could see that there were no crocodiles, so by far the best route to avoid being seen would be by water. He gently lowered himself into the Nile.

Moments later, he was scrambling up the muddy bank onto the island and was pleased to see he was only a few metres away from the prison boat. It was completely unguarded. *Ay must have fixed that*, Freddie thought. Freddie crouched on its deck, panting and dripping. Four desperate faces turned in alarm and the small girl looked like she was about to cry out. Freddie put his finger to his lips and the father, sensing that Freddie was there to help and not hurt, gently covered the girl's mouth and calmed her with a few soft words. Freddie pulled the knife slowly from his belt and set about sawing and cutting the thick knots that held the cage tightly shut. It was sapping Freddie's strength and, as he started on the second knot, the man beckoned to him to take over for a while. Freddie was glad of the rest and took back the knife again midway through the third and final fastening.

There were suddenly raised voices in the distance as the last threads were severed. Freddie ushered the family over the side of the boat, into the water to hide in the shadows. There was still a glimmer of daylight, too much for an escape. Freddie tried to explain in Egyptian but the family spoke only their native tongue. So Freddie mimed: *sun going down – dark – run away.*

Further along the shoreline, a lurking figure hopped from one boat to the next. Tuta made his jerky way towards the prison barge as Freddie signalled to the family to duck down under the water as he passed. Freddie cautiously observed the killer's progress. A minute later, Tuta retraced his steps. He looked angry that Rudjek had apparently got to the family before him.

The family began to wade ashore, but Freddie stopped them. It was still too light and he knew Rudjek would be along soon to try to do the same as Tuta. Freddie held them back and signed: *one more man, knife, wait.*

Five long minutes passed. Suddenly, a man jumped down onto the sandy mud in front of the five bobbing heads. It was Rudjek, the short, squat soldier who Freddie had mistrusted from the first. He moved stealthily to the prison boat, a short sword in his hand, which occasionally caught the light from flaming torches.

But a moment later, he, too, made his way back and away from the prisoners' cage, naturally assuming that Tuta had beaten him to the task. The small girl coughed slightly as water had got up her nose, and the world stopped. The noise of Rudjek's feet climbing up the side of the barque next to them paused. Freddie watched as Rudjek peered over the side into the darkness, looking for anything unusual before giving up and moving away. Freddie counted to ten, then navigated his small band between the boats well away from the shoreline, until at the end of the convoy they spilled onto the island and into the cover of some waist-high rushes.

A hundred metres along the muddy shore, a fishing skiff stood out in silhouette. Using the undergrowth as cover, the five figures moved silently until they were level with the boat. The man checked its seaworthiness. It was made of strong papyrus reeds tied together with twine and had two oars safely stowed on its flat top.

They carried the skiff to the water and both children were loaded aboard. The mother took up one oar and the father the other. He stopped and clasped Freddie's hands in heartfelt thanks before they slipped into the current and away to safety, to start a new life in this land of beauty, horror and now, kindness. The last thing Freddie saw of them was a huge smile from the little girl, who waved before turning and looking ahead at whatever was to come.

Ay would no doubt find that the prisoners had escaped when he questioned Tuta and Rudjek. At least the family would be far away by that time. But Ay would know that someone was operating against him.

A slight breeze lifted the palm fronds of surrounding trees and Freddie sat for a while watching the torches of the flotilla and the lights of the distant palace as it shimmered in the starry night.

He had one mission left and it would be the most dangerous thing he had ever attempted.

The next afternoon, they gathered safely on the west bank at Meidum, where a huge five-stepped colossus of a pyramid dominated the surrounding landscape. It was an amazing sight, but it looked in a terrible state of repair, almost close to collapsing.

Userhat's barque was moored alongside Freddie's barge, and well after dark, the unmistakable figure of Ay again visited his accomplices. The guttering flame of his torch illuminated the gaunt-faced man as he glided silently across the deck. Freddie crawled close by and witnessed Ay give Tuta a ring from his left hand. The latter looked a little surprised but said only, "Thank you, great lord. I was expecting my reward after my second commission."

"It's to keep you focused. A good job was done. From what Rudjek told me, you were the first to the prisoners. It was clever to make it look like they had escaped. I am impressed, and as for their actual fate, I shall leave that between you and the gods. Your work is half done."

He slunk away as silently as he'd arrived, leaving a bemused Tuta much the richer but none the wiser. Userhat snatched the ring from him and said, "I'll keep that safe until your next job is finished, *then* you will have your full reward."

Freddie shuddered and thought he understood exactly what that reward might be. Userhat was a seething knot of treachery and could not be trusted. He placed the ring on his bony finger and it jangled against the others. He was acquiring quite a collection.

Chapter 15

Freddie was awake long before dawn for the race to Giza. Soldiers, sailors, servants and officials had all been away from their Memphis homes for much longer than expected due to Kha's chariot accident. The thought of their home city spurred them on.

The unbelievable sight of the pyramids at Giza slowly grew larger and larger. Freddie couldn't believe his eyes. Even though they were well away from the western bank of the Nile, they were still enormous and Freddie couldn't wait to get close.

Immediately after dark, Freddie jumped ship and waded ashore. It was just as well as several of the supply barges were floated away minutes later. A full moon provided plenty of light, and the silhouettes of the pyramids were as good a target to hike to as anyone could ask for. He was cold despite the vigorous exercise because of the wet clothes clinging to him. But he had to carry on and reach the temple before dawn to be in position to deliver a very special message to two friends who thought he was dead.

Twice he had to hide as small convoys of chariots, carts and servants rushed past in the night, obviously on their way to prepare the temple for the royal arrival.

As he got closer, the huge shapes of the pyramids dominated his view; vast, dark shapes against the bright starry sky. Freddie had to make for the temple of the sphinx where the ceremony was to be held. It wasn't hard to find as that's where the hub of activity was. There was nothing for it but to be brave and venture closer so he could find a hiding place. But it had to be somewhere he could get a message to Kha or Ankha.

In the dark, no one could tell he was a mousey-haired Albanical teenager, as everyone had their heads swathed to ward off the cold. Baskets of bread and fruit were stacked awaiting the morning and Freddie helped himself to some figs, grapes and bread and decided to climb the 15-metre outside wall of the temple to get up high, away from people and to spot a safe place. The walls were made of huge blocks of roughly hewn stone so there were plenty of footholds. In places, it was powdery, and once or twice trickles of debris came away in his fingers and skittered to the ground below. Each time he froze against the wall, hoping the noise hadn't given him away, but the hubbub of preparation elsewhere easily drowned out his climb.

He reached the top, and to his surprise he saw there was no roof covering the rectangular space. Two central rows of pillars supported broad, stone crossbeams about ten metres above the temple floor; a sort of open latticework. There was an altar at the pyramid end and two additional smaller open chambers, one on each side.

Freddie was easily hidden up here as the crossbeams were easily a metre and a half wide. Although high up, he felt secure. He crawled all the way round and realised that he had complete access to the whole temple. Alerting his friends was now his only thought and, as he waited in the dark, he felt for Kha's scarab around his neck to check it was safe.

Some time later, still in the dead of night, music wafted towards Freddie from the Nile. Ceremonial horns were accompanied by regular drumbeats. It was the familiar marching music that heralded the approaching guests and the royal party. Freddie peered at the preparations as more torches were lit and the magical open interior of the temple transformed into what looked like a film set.

Priests and nobility in all their finery began lining the centre of the space and took up prominent positions. Freddie eventually spotted Kha and Ankha approaching. Even in the relative darkness, Kha's golden clothes shimmered and sparkled as the light from the torches reflected off them.

Kha was led to the left side-chamber of the temple and Ankha to the right. They were hidden from the throng by beautiful embroidered curtains, but Freddie could see everything perfectly from his perch high above.

In the east, the light just above the horizon turned from midnight to royal, then sky blue. Not long now. The shapes of the surrounding landscape became defined. Freddie turned and was absolutely stunned to see the fragile first half-light touch the face of a man. Half human, half lion and made of hundreds of tons of stone. With every second, the light brought out more detail of the huge sphinx and the colossal pyramids behind it. It seemed to be smiling at him.

"Right, concentrate. I'm not a tourist. I have a job to do," Freddie told himself.

He carefully worked his way round to a point high above Ankha. Only Kyky and Nedjem were with her now and they stood ready by the curtain waiting for a signal and not looking at their queen. It was now or never.

Freddie retrieved the scarab, then made several practice lobs with his arms to make sure his sleeve wouldn't restrict him. Then, hoping his aim was true, he gently released the beautiful turquoise beetle into the air. It descended in an arc, brushing Ankha's sleeve and falling perfectly in the rough dust at her feet. The touch of the scarab on her sleeve alarmed her and she pulled her arm away and gasped. Kyky turned and asked if all was well, and Ankha staring disbelievingly at the ground, lifted her head and nodded to her maid.

When Kyky turned again to her duties Ankha bent quickly, retrieved the scarab in her right hand and as subtly as her emotions would allow she gently raised her disbelieving eyes upwards and caught sight of a valiant mousey-haired guardian They smiled at each other and Freddie saw tears of joy spring to Ankha's eyes.

The moment was only broken when the curtains were swept aside and Kha and Ankha walked their separate paths to the centre of the temple to stand before the altar. They turned and Ankha took Kha's hand in hers. For a second he looked bemused, but then his face lit up in the most extraordinary smile as he felt the scarab encased between their palms.

The sun peered over the horizon, streaked through the open eastern end of the temple and splashed its light on them both. The dramatic effect of the sunlight on their golden robes was unforgettable. It bounced off them in shards of reflected light and was the single most magical moment Freddie had ever experienced. Why would you not worship someone who quite literally burst into golden light before your very eyes.

King Tutankhamun and queen Ankhesenamun were ablaze in a glorious golden beam, which was not quite as broad as the beam on Kha's smiling face or that of his queen or, indeed, that of their loyal guardian, Freddie Malone.

Chapter 16

Freddie watched the day unfold, covering himself against the ferocious heat of the sun. He saw a tented village spring up diagonally to the left of the sphinx and the royal couple retreat to its safety.

As the sun travelled in a long arc overhead, Freddie's attention turned to his meeting with Ankha. He looked around for the largest man-made object. It didn't take long. Diagonally right from the temple stood the Great Pyramid of Khufu, which completely dominated the surrounding area. Even the mighty sphinx looked a little small in comparison.

Just in front of the great stone structure, three smaller pyramids had been built in a line. Freddie thought he could watch for Ankha's approach from there. The danger time was after the feast, so he had to speak to Ankha long before that.

The sky darkened and a wonderful sunset began behind the pyramid to Freddie's left. It cast a huge triangular shadow towards him, with a blazing red, orange and then pink light show framing its silhouette.

Freddie carefully descended the temple wall. In the dying light, he could see a new set of guards relieving the men who had stood watch during the long, hot afternoon.

Attention was focused elsewhere, just as Kha had said it would be, and it was easy for Freddie to scuttle the 200 metres to the farthest of the three small pyramids, the far side of which was now almost completely dark. The ground was uneven, barren and dusty. Freddie found a low pit providing cover and a perfect viewpoint. How long would he have to wait?

His stomach rumbled, reminding him that he hadn't eaten since before dawn. He was feeling tired and dehydrated. He simply rested his head on his forearm and within a minute or so he was asleep.

He dreamed of crocodiles and temples, assassins and sunlight, papyrus skiffs and royal barques. Suddenly he awoke in a frozen panic. How long had he been asleep? What if he'd missed Ankha? What an idiot he was! He had one thing to do and his weakness had jeopardised everything.

From his left there was movement. A shambling shape in rags, carrying a reed basket, shuffled noisily along the base of the great pyramid. Freddie feared

Kha might already lie murdered. He turned to see if he could see the feast beyond the line of small pyramids, the old crone sat heavily on a rock near the base of the giant structure. She gathered her breath and started to sing gently and quietly. Freddie strained to hear. The old woman was bent almost double so that she was facing the ground. But it was no old woman. Freddie recognised the voice and the song. It was Ankha!

Freddie raced to her side and in a second her headdress was removed and the glorious Queen Ankhesenamun's beautiful smile greeted him.

"You live! We can't believe it. When the scarab landed at my feet I burst with joy. Kha is happier than I have ever seen him. He has been crying for days. We thought something strange was happening when the prisoner's cage was found empty. Was—"

"It was me, I released them, they're safe."

"How did you—?"

But Freddie interrupted. There was no time to explain all of that now, time was running out.

"Ankha I must warn you. There is another plot. After the feast tonight there will be a man hiding in your tent. And when Kha goes to sleep he will strike. Surround yourselves with Parennefer's guards and search your tent. Under Ay's instructions, a man called Tuta is being smuggled in by Rudjek, who is definitely a traitor, be careful of him. Please! Remember, the killer's name is Tuta."

"How do you know all this?"

"I have been keeping my eyes and ears open." He smiled modestly and looked around.

"You are the best friend anyone could have, Freddie Malone. Kha and I thank you again. We will find a way to return you to our side in Memphis. So I give you the scarab again as it has proved a good signal. Remember that it must be with Kha when his time comes to travel to the next world. That is where it lives, guarding his safe passage to Osiris." She pressed the turquoise beetle into Freddie's hand.

Ankha lifted her basket and revealed water in an earthenware jug, fish, fruit and a small beautiful necklace.

"Use these precious stones to buy food and shelter in the coming weeks. If you run out, Kyky will be at the palace gates at each full moon and can give you more or lead you secretly to us."

"Thank you so much," said Freddie, eagerly drinking the much-needed water.

"We hope soon to be rid of Ay. A future with him is too horrible to consider. Please find out what you can. When this killer is revealed tonight, be close by so you can identify Ay as the man who arranged it all."

"But it will be my word against his. No one will believe me."

"Let's see what happens. Be close by and do what's best – for you and for us. We are so glad you're alive. I can't tell you how important you are to us." And with that the great queen of Egypt broke down into silent sobs.

"You must return for the feast," Freddie said.

"I am fully dressed under these rags. No one took any notice of me as I walked here. Let's hope it's the same as I go back. Watch for me."

"I will."

"Remember, the scarab must finish its travels with Kha on the foot of his sarcophagus. Either you or I must put it there if anything terrible happens to him. Promise me that?"

"Of course I promise, but that will be years away. I will return the scarab as soon as we are rid of Ay."

She smiled, wrapped her head in the rags and skipped nimbly away until, at the corner of the great pyramid, she turned, waved at Freddie and resumed her old-lady walk across the open ground towards the tented village. Freddie's eyes followed her until she was swallowed in darkness. As no great shouts of alarm were heard, he presumed she had managed a safe return.

Movement to his right turned his head and he was sure he just caught a glimpse of a black cloak swirl around the next corner of the pyramid. Again he had that strange sensation that the vortex was near and he was being watched. But it was impossible, surely. The vortex was hundreds of kilometres away near Waset.

How am I going to get back to Waset and the portal? This thought preoccupied him for some time.

Music began, torches were lit and servants guided guests to a huge collection of large cushions scattered on the ground in front of the middle pyramid. The guests seated themselves and were served wine and fruit. Freddie climbed up the back of the sphinx where he could see both the feast and the royal quarters.

Kha and Ankha were led to the festivities, where they sat more formally at a table with ten or so dignitaries. Freddie concentrated on Kha's tent. Nothing was going to happen at the feast, but he wanted to spot anyone acting suspiciously.

He didn't have long to wait as, from down on his left, two shapes moved quickly and quietly across the ground in a straight line heading for the rear of the makeshift village. Rudjek and Tuta were shrouded in dark cloaks and Freddie had to peer very hard into the night to keep up with their progress. But it was clear Ay's plan was in motion. Freddie breathed a huge sigh of relief that his sleep hadn't lasted longer and he'd been able to tell Ankha all about the plot. He started down from the lion's back.

The feast ended and the royal party stood and processed back the way they had come. The unmistakable shape of Parennefer and forty soldiers marched alongside the royal couple. Ay looked about himself nervously and, as the group stood outside

143

the royal tent, Kha gave the order for Parennefer to search. Freddie was nearby now, but stayed back in the shadows.

He heard Ay protest, "Don't you think my men will have done that? Why suddenly do you want it done again?"

"There is treachery afoot, Lord Ay," said Kha plainly. "We are made aware of another plot on the throne – search thoroughly, leave nothing untouched."

Ay began to fidget and then from nowhere the oily Userhat joined him by his side. They whispered nervously to each other and Userhat nodded, then dissolved into the darkness again.

Parennefer and five men had entered the tent and within a minute came back out dragging the figure of Tuta behind them. He was silent and emotionless as they threw his knife into the dust.

Kha looked immediately at Ay, who lowered his gaze. A cool, clear voice rang out. It was Ankha.

"Who has promised you wealth for killing the living son of Amun? Tell us now in the safe knowledge it will not only be you who pays the ultimate price for such treachery."

Tuta shifted under the restraint of three guards.

"Who?" asked Kha in a louder, more agitated voice. Tuta was a vicious man and he wasn't going to give in to questioning by teenagers even if one of them was a living god. Ay shifted nervously and looked around.

Freddie followed his gaze and before he had time to shout out, an arrow flew through the air and sunk deep into Tuta's chest. He died without a sound.

Guards instantly surrounded Kha and Ankha. Freddie ran towards where the arrow had been fired. He took the retreating Userhat by surprise, and rugby-tackled him to the ground. Everyone saw the disturbance and a surprised Ay shouted, "Take him! Take the boy! It was him! He fired the arrow. I saw it. Userhat, stop him escaping!"

There was nothing for it but for Freddie to run. Ay's soldiers were already advancing towards him. Instinctively, Freddie started to recite his homeward mantra. He knew it was probably useless but it had rescued him before. As he ran away he started reciting 'If—' as fast as he could. Between gulps of air he shot across the ground and babbled great chunks of the poem to the ink-black night. He was heading for the sphinx and the temple. He thought if the vortex didn't open, he could hide there, but the soldiers were closing on him and he still had a verse to go.

"If you can talk with crowds and keep your virtue,
Or walk with Kings—"

He suddenly realised he was running away from his friends but that Kha's life had been saved again, thanks to him. He would find a way back, he had to. He had the scarab! On and on he ran.

"Yours is the Earth and everything that's in it,

And – which is more – you'll be a Man, my son!"

A surge of wind swept across the desert, flinging dust and grit sideways at Freddie. As he approached the moat around the sphinx, a dark, hooded figure appeared in front of him. Freddie instantly recognised it as one of the demons from the vortex.

"You have what's mine!" the apparition shouted, as Freddie approached at top speed. The soldiers thundered on in pursuit. He sidestepped the hooded figure as he reached the moat's edge and darted away from its outstretched arms. Freddie's momentum took him over the ditch towards the back of the sphinx, whose solid stone haunch now miraculously turned into a portal. Accompanied by a sound like an aircraft's roar, Freddie surged through the magical opening and sped his way back along the winding vortex. All the way he was surrounded by the grey-cloaked spirits, who escorted him back to safety. Remembering to go feet first so he didn't land on his head, he flopped through the wall at the end of the tunnel as it conveniently opened into his bedroom.

He was home. He was exhausted, but he was safe. In his securely held rucksack was the scarab of King Tutankhamun, nearly three-and-a-half thousand years from where it should be!

Chapter 17

Connor was speechless and simply smiled in the silence that followed, as the wonder of Freddie's adventure hung in the air.

Ruby toyed with her trainer laces as if slightly bored.

"You got the history wrong, buddy. You'll have to rewrite all that Ankha stuff. She married Ay. I told you. What's the point of me doing all that research and you just ignoring it?"

"Yes, sorry, Ruby," Freddie replied. "I'll write it properly when the—"

"Good! All right, I forgive you," Ruby interrupted. "Other than that, it was brilliant. You, buddy, are a natural, and don't tell anyone I said this, but that story was cool. I'm hungry."

They pooled their resources and devoured a

strange and varied feast of tuna sandwiches from Freddie, vegetarian couscous wraps from Ruby, and cheese and onion crisps and chocolate wafers from Connor. Connor stopped mid-bite as a terrifying thought suddenly flashed through his mind.

"What about the scarab? You need to get the scarab back to Kha. He can't get to Ossie—"

"Osiris!" interrupted Ruby once again. "Weren't you listening, Conman?"

"Yeah, Osiris. That's it. Kha needs it back."

Freddie shot a look to Connor as if it was a subject best dealt with when they were alone. Connor felt a heat rush to his cheeks.

"It's easy, just throw the scarab to Ankha after the tattoo guy gets the arrow, before you jump on Userhat," Ruby suggested, confidently.

"That's good, yeah. That's what I'll do. Good thinking, Ruby," Freddie quickly agreed.

Connor blushed and blew out a silent stream of air. He'd nearly done it again. He made up his mind he wasn't going to say anymore until he and Freddie were alone. He comforted himself with the last two chocolate wafers from the packet.

They all agreed that in order to finish the story they needed to do more research. That was best done at the library as the three of them couldn't all look up different things on one battered laptop.

Fifteen minutes later they were standing on the

library steps. Whilst Ruby called her mum to explain where she was, Freddie and Connor whispered a hurried emergency plan.

"I'm going to look for stuff about his tomb," said Freddie, "and the areas around the portals. Why don't you do the pyramids, sphinx and Memphis, err – Cairo."

Connor nodded, pleased to be given an important job. "No probs."

"Remember, it's 1328 BC. We want maps and details for Kha's reign in the Eighteenth Dynasty. People. Names."

"Right, I'll give it a go."

"Give what a go?" enquired Ruby returning to the group. "My mum says I can stay till five. Give what a go?"

Freddie grinned at his best friend.

"It's going to be difficult finding maps of things from 1328 BC, but if anyone can track them down, it'll be Connor."

"Well – I—" Connor mumbled shyly.

"Go for it, Conman! Do your stuff!" said Ruby, "I'm concentrating on Ankha, coz she's got a pretty weird old story. Let's go."

Every book on Egypt gave different dates for Kha's reign. Who should they believe? One thing they all said was that he died before he was twenty, and that he may have been killed. Some said he had a disease called spina bifida, others said he had epilepsy.

Ay did succeed Kha and ruled for four years, and he did marry Ankha. She had tried to marry Zannanza, the son of the Hittite king, but he was murdered on his way to Egypt. Horemheb was pharaoh after Ay. And Ay *did* swap his tomb with Kha for some reason. Kha was buried in tomb 62 in the East Valley.

By mid-afternoon, Freddie's battered notebook, which had already been to ancient Egypt once, was crammed full of drawings, dimensions, facts and figures. Freddie and Connor sent silent texts, swapping information they didn't want Ruby to know. After all, to her, this was just a project. Everything was going really well until through the doors of the library – and at full volume – came Finnegan, Kathleen and a slightly flustered Uncle Patrick.

They had been out shopping for replacement batteries for their hearing aids, which ordinarily would have been something for everyone to celebrate, but they had decided to divert to the library as Finnegan had a complaint about his new library card.

Their entrance caused a real stir, and the initial patience the harassed lady librarian offered soon dissolved as her inner steel locked horns with

Finnegan. With Uncle Patrick as referee, the two opposing factions increased their volume and Kathleen found a seat. She could see this was going to be a long one.

Connor could see that Patrick, for once, seemed to be floundering. He was concentrating his efforts on trying to stop Finnegan's bad language and had so far failed.

Freddie sank in his chair, trying to hide behind a large book about the Valley of the Kings. Connor sat open-mouthed, and Ruby joined the others in the library who were 'sshushing' the disruptive old man.

The manager relieved the weakening librarian, who looked exhausted. But even the manager soon caved in, and a temporary card was issued with great haste.

Finnegan paraded around, exclaiming to the packed library why he was in the right.

Then his eyes fell on Connor, whose heart sank to new depths with a jolt. It was as if someone had poured petrol on a bonfire.

"... And there's never any room to sit down. Look at that boy, taking up the space of three people. He shouldn't be allowed in here. He'll break the furniture!"

Uncle Patrick stepped in assertively. "Be quiet, now, Finn, don't talk to Connor that way. You've got your card, now choose a book and let's go."

"He's too fat for a library," continued Finnegan. "Look at—"

"How dare you! Oi! You! How dare you!" A voice cut through the supercharged atmosphere. Finnegan turned his attention to the girl with blue hair. He breathed deeply, ready to bombard this new adversary with a choice selection of insults.

"I wouldn't say another word if I were you," Ruby blasted. "You're an embarrassment, and I've got it all recorded on my phone, so unless you want me to share your behaviour on social media, I'd stop now if I were you."

The room was silent. All eyes shot back to Finnegan. He opened his mouth to reply but Ruby continued. "And how dare you talk to my friend like that? What's he ever done to you? You're no oil painting yourself! Get your book and leave the rest of us in peace. We've got work to do."

A cheer and then a round of applause swept the large room. Ruby sat down and picked up her pencil to write, despite her hand shaking a little.

Finnegan stood alone in the middle of the room. His face was red with fury and little flecks of white spittle dotted the corners of his mouth. Uncle Patrick approached him and placed a hand firmly on Finnegan's back and ushered the defeated old man meekly away to the door. On the way, he paused to collect Kathleen. She accepted his other arm and said at full volume, "What's social media? Never heard of it!"

Connor stared straight ahead. He knew if he blinked, the tears that were brimming would cascade on to the extensive notes he'd made about ancient Egyptian recipes. He didn't know if the tears were because of Finnegan's vile insults, or Ruby's incredible show of defence.

Freddie couldn't have sat any lower in his seat without slipping onto the floor. He shuffled quietly upwards again, mortified it hadn't been him who'd stood up for his best friend. He looked at Ruby's pencil scrawl. She had written the same words over and over again.

Just keep writing. Look busy. Just keep writing. Look busy.

The library settled. Everyone who was there would remember the events, but there were three friends for whom the future was set. There was now a fierce loyalty between them. Freddie felt that out of the crazy scene an unbreakable bond had been forged that would last forever. He felt as stunned and speechless as Connor still looked.

"That's what happens when you stand up for something you believe in. The world changes. It may be a little change or it may be a huge change. The important thing is to stand up!" Uncle Patrick said later in the car.

Patrick had driven Finnegan and Kathleen home and come straight back to give the three friends a lift home to Normandy Avenue.

Connor walked like a zombie behind Freddie and Ruby towards the library exit. He was disconcerted at the sympathetic stares he received and busied himself sorting the pink waste paper notes held tightly in his sweaty hands. Without thinking, he dumped them in the bin by the photocopier, along with his useless first attempts at maps, doodles and sweet wrappers. Uncle Patrick ushered them into his car like a posh chauffeur.

As they drove away, Connor noticed Jasper and Kelvin emerge from the library and stand on the front steps, staring into Kelvin's carrier bag. *Oh! No. Did they hear what Finnegan had said? That would be a disaster.* He didn't want to think about those two right now.

Freddie and Ruby had both given him a consoling pat on the shoulder on the short car ride home, but Connor didn't speak. He was still in shock.

As Uncle Patrick drove off into the fading afternoon light, the three friends made arrangements to meet in the park the next day. Ruby turned back after having walked away. She ran at Connor and gave him an enormous hug.

"Good on you, Conman. Respect. Don't let

him bother you. See you two randoms tomorrow."

"Thank you, Ruby," Connor gently called after her, as she pushed open her front gate.

"No probs. See you tomoz."

With Mrs M calling from the doorway, the boys stood awkwardly for a second before fist bumping and going their separate ways. Freddie called after Connor.

"See you tomorrow, mate. Sorry about—"

"Yeah. No probs. See you tomoz," parroted Connor, knowing that he now worshipped the ground Ruby walked on. He couldn't wait for 'tomoz'.

Chapter 18

Connor slept badly. So many conflicting emotions were buzzing around his weary brain. He lay watching the dawn creep into his bedroom and felt exhausted rather than excited by the day ahead. He got up early and searched the kitchen for provisions, but found nothing that would lift his mood, so he dragged himself towards the park.

As he emerged from the newsagent opposite the main gates, his heart skipped a beat. There was Ruby. She was laughing with someone, her bright sapphire eyes sparkling in the morning sunshine. Then, surprisingly, Kelvin emerged from the doorway of the hairdresser's. He was clutching his usual carrier bag and had a confident swagger Connor hadn't seen before. What on earth was Ruby doing with Kelvin?

Ruby laughed again at something Kelvin said and shook her head. Kelvin put the bag on the ground and delved inside. He pulled out a handful of paper. Distinctive, pink paper notes. The ones from the library. Connor's world started spinning. He went cold with fear and felt light-headed. Kelvin offered one half of a chocolate bar to Ruby, who again shook her head.

Ruby turned her back and Connor couldn't see what was going on. *Was she a spy? Had she infiltrated on a mission from Jasper? Did she even live next door to Freddie?* Of course she did! He knew that. Connor stopped himself from having any more wild thoughts. He was predicting a catastrophe when there was no evidence. He needed to calm down. Maybe there was nothing in it. But Freddie had told Ruby all about Kelvin, and where he fitted in to the whole problem with Jasper.

The two of them talked for a minute or so more, then Ruby waved and crossed the road to the park. Connor needed to tell Freddie what he'd seen, but Ruby was already deep in conversation with Freddie when he arrived. He would have to be clever and extract any important information without alerting her. Then Connor remembered he had seen Jasper and Kelvin with the bag on the library steps as Uncle Patrick drove them away, but he hadn't had the mental energy at that moment to really register it. Had those two been listening? Connor had thrown the notes away himself and Ruby was ahead of him at that moment... *Unless she'd gone back?* His mind kept throwing up more questions.

And now Connor wouldn't be able to talk to Freddie alone. He tried to remember everything he'd tossed into the library bin. He took a deep breath and felt sick as he remembered the doodle he'd drawn. It was of the map – and it had a hole in it with a pair of feet sticking out of Egypt. Surely Kelvin wouldn't know what that signified. What else was there? After Finnegan's outburst, Connor had been in such a daze he barely remembered leaving. The Memphis map! He'd thrown away his first two rubbish attempts. He shuddered and mentally listed all the things Kelvin might have his hands on:

1. Doodle of Freddie's map – with feet disappearing into Egypt.

2. Two bad attempts at map of Memphis.

3. He had doodled the first two lines of 'If—' whilst waiting for Freddie to finish with the atlas.

He swallowed and wondered how Freddie was going to take the news that he might have compromised everything, again.

"You're quiet, Conman," Ruby commented. There was a relaxed friendliness to her tone. Was it all an act? Connor was seeing her in a completely different light now.

"Yeah I'm, y'know I'm—" He swept his already neat hair away from his forehead nervously.

"Thinking about 'stuff', I bet," she helped out, smiling supportively.

"Yeah. Thinking about stuff," he agreed distantly. Ruby didn't seem to notice, but Freddie immediately sensed Connor's mood. Something was up.

Overnight, Freddie had been thinking long and hard about Ruby. She had more than proved herself yesterday, standing up for Connor, and she was fun and clever. If they could just curb her natural tendency to want to lead the group, that would be great. They didn't need a leader, they all just needed to agree. At least it seemed their secrets were safe for now. Ruby thought it was all a story and she didn't believe in the map's magical properties.

"Let's prepare as if all three of us are going back to Egypt to return the scarab," said Freddie.

"Yeah!" Ruby enthused, "That's great! Let's finish Egypt first. My space adventure can wait."

Connor threw himself into the charade. He tried to push his suspicions about Ruby away, but they kept returning like a boomerang. One minute he was enthralled by her, the next, he was guarded, in case she was a double agent. Freddie kept an eye on his friend and made a note to check on him later.

Then Freddie's phone rang. It was his mum, saying that she and Mr M had to drop everything and look after Kathleen and Finnegan. The old man wouldn't get out of bed, was not eating and Uncle Patrick was away.

"There's food in the fridge, enough for Connor and Ruby if you want. But you've got to come home now, as I'm leaving the key out. Are you listening? Come home now and I'll leave the front door key under the recycling bin. OK? I don't want to leave it there more than a few minutes. If you go out, you must lock up. Promise me, Freddie."

"I promise, Mum."

"We'll be back by teatime. I'm sorry to spoil your day, darlin'. I'll ring from Finnegan's in an hour. Start walking home now."

The trio walked quickly back to Freddie's.

Kelvin was on his way to Jasper's HQ in the mall when Mrs Malone cut straight across his path. He could sense she was in a panic. Maybe it was something to do with Freddie? It was worth him checking out. Jasper was always hungry for any information about Freddie, and Kelvin was always keen to provide it. He'd been doing well in that department recently.

Jeanette Malone was like a tornado whirling around the supermarket. Kelvin observed her from behind the tills and guessed rightly that she would come through the self-service channel. Mrs M thrust item after item through the scanner and flicked her long, dark hair behind her ears as she bent down to bag them. She put her hand in her coat pocket to get her credit card from her purse, which she produced along with a set of keys.

"Oh no!" she exclaimed loudly, causing startled looks from people around her.

The woman supervising the self-service tills stepped forwards. "Can I help you, love?"

"No, it's – aaagghh! I've got my keys! I mean, I'm meant to have left them!" As she grabbed at the heavy carrier bag, a handle broke and some onions and potatoes spilled onto the floor. Kelvin, sensing his chance, rushed to her aid. He scrambled around on the tiled floor picking up the loose vegetables. He looked up to see the flustered lady with her mane of black hair smiling down at him.

"Thank you! You're a darlin' boy."

"Are you Freddie's mum? Freddie Malone, I mean."

"Yes! Do you go to school with Freddie?"

"Yes. He and Connor are… my two best friends."

"Ooh! What's your name, darling'? I've got to

rush. I'll tell them you helped me."

"My name's Ke—" he stopped. "Err – King! Ben King."

"Well, Ben, you're a star. I've got to fly."

Kelvin suddenly felt a flash of inspiration.

"I'm going to see Connor this afternoon, I've rescued his homework. He lost it and I'm taking it to him. I think he's in the park."

"No, Ben, he's at our house."

"Oh! Is there a problem with your keys?"

"Oooh, yes! Look, be a love and take them to Freddie, would you? That'll save me rushin' back there right now. They won't be able to get in otherwise. Do you know Normandy Avenue, Number 10? They're there now. I'll text them and let them know you've got the keys and are on your way. They'll give you some lunch, I expect."

"It's all right, I'll text Connor," Kelvin offered, already tapping a message into his phone. "Look, there. It's done. OK?" He made a play of pressing send and pocketed his phone.

"Wonderful," said Mrs M, gathering her broken bag under her arm. Then she handed over a crazy collection of animals, trolls, labels and tags interspersed with lots of keys.

"You're a darlin' boy, Ben. Hmm... Ben King? No, Freddie and Connor haven't talked about you, but they're always in a world of their own those two. You'll go there now, will you?"

"Yes. Yes I'm on my way. Goodbye, Mrs Malone, it's been very nice meeting you."

"And you too, Ben. Bye now!" And with that she headed to the side doors where Mr M was illegally parked.

Kelvin couldn't believe it. He didn't quite know *what* he'd done. He hadn't even really planned it. But a kind of miracle had happened. He pondered his next move. He had a choice. He could take the keys to Freddie, return Connor's notes, and maybe in gratitude be accepted as a lifelong friend of theirs. Or he could go back to the dark side.

After he'd deleted the message to Connor that he'd pretended to send, Kelvin got on the escalator to the third floor and Jasper's usual hang-out, overlooking the whole mall. He could sense the laser stares of the gang as he approached. Surely this was worth a lifetime's membership? Maybe, as a reward, he'd be promoted to Jasper's No. 2. He felt he had gold dust in his possession.

Freddie and Connor hadn't been able to find the keys, but they were safely in the house anyway. Ruby had pulled them both up onto the kitchen extension and from there they got in through his bedroom window.

Freddie called his mum to say all was well, but he went straight to voicemail because she was ringing him at the same time to tell him that they'd had to divert to the hospital. Finnegan had just been taken in by ambulance. He was very unwell.

It was a message Freddie didn't hear for a very long time.

Chapter 19

Ruby was back out on the flat roof yelling down to her brothers in the garden next door. Connor and Freddie took advantage of her absence to check their rucksacks. Notebook with tomb details, vocabulary for Connor to learn, maps, torches, a multi-tool, camera and sun cream.

"The necklace!" hissed Freddie, quickly retrieving it from inside a pair of shoes in his wardrobe.

"I've got my PE kit like you said," Connor told him, pulling a very stretchy T-shirt and shorts out of a side pocket. "And white trainers and sandals."

"Great, the palace will kit you out properly. It's just for the first day or so."

Freddie checked under his bed for his folded Egyptian clothes: his shendyt, tunic top, head-wrap and sandals. Connor touched the thick, strong fabric. His heart started thumping. It *was* going to happen, he knew it.

Freddie shoved his phone into the zip-up pouch to ensure he had it this time. Then they stuffed their rucksacks back into the cupboard, on top of the rope, which Freddie thought they would need to get down the pipe tunnel. Connor had decided not to tell Freddie about Ruby's meeting with Kelvin. He felt he still needed some kind of proof. He was too late anyway, as she climbed through the window laughing, "Did you punks miss me?"

The truth, from Connor's point of view, was 'Yes'. He felt his cheeks go red, a little jump of nerves in his stomach and a slight catch in his voice. But he had to make sure of her loyalties. He felt terrible, doubting her after the way she'd defended him yesterday. *This is complicated!* he thought.

Ruby set to work on Freddie's laptop, scanning pages from the internet. All of a sudden the boys fell silent. Freddie's skin prickled with anticipation as he felt the atmosphere begin to change, like the loaded seconds before a thunderstorm. The hairs on his legs, arms and neck stood on end. He looked at Connor, who sat on the bed with a glazed look of bewilderment on his face. Connor could feel it too.

Ruby was fixated on the computer so she didn't notice Niagara Falls begin to leak a little. She didn't see Neptune turn and smile, or the three pyramids race each other around Africa like Formula One cars. But Freddie did. He flinched. Suddenly the idea of taking his friends back three-and-a-half thousand years didn't seem such a marvellous idea. He knew *he* was protected by the power of the vortex, but what about his companions? He looked at Connor again, whose mouth dropped open as he once again observed the mischief on the map. What if they hated it and wanted to return immediately? Freddie could look after himself, but being responsible for them was different. Doubts and fears whizzed around his brain and he felt the need to calmly close his eyes and just breathe.

All was silent in the room.

Then a creak sounded on the staircase outside.

"Both the front and back doors are locked, aren't they?" whispered Freddie. Connor pulled a face.

"Yeah. They've got to be. Why?"

Freddie took a deep breath, "I think we're about to—"

Another louder creak on the stairs.

Ruby looked up from the laptop. "What was that?"

Freddie frowned. "I don't know. Connor, can you get the rucksacks and the rope, please?" he said, trying to sound as normal as possible whilst wildly panicking inside. He began swapping his clothes for his Egyptian kit, as Connor headed back from the wardrobe with terror in his eyes.

"Here you go. Are we...?" stuttered Connor.

"What are you two randoms yabbering about?" Ruby turned and saw Freddie emerge in his Egyptian clothes from behind Connor, who had the rope and both rucksacks grasped in front of him like a shield. The two boys then sat facing the map, perched awkwardly on the end of Freddie's bed.

"Oh! Brilliant, are we re-enacting it? That's cool. I haven't got a costume. I could use a sheet!"

"Never mind, Ruby, you have my bag. Hold on to it tightly," Freddie told her. "Sit next to Connor. Remember, whatever happens, stick together and don't panic. Here, grab hold of the rope."

Ruby opened her mouth to reply but stopped when all their attention was taken by the cautious testing of the door handle. As it began to turn, an electrical spark shot from the map to the door. Freddie had never seen this happen before. Coloured lights flashed on and off like a disco. A church organ started playing and got quickly louder as other noises joined in. Singing, violins, hammers hitting metal, chainsaws, drums, aircraft engines, TV soaps blared, as well as shouts and sirens, all overlapping and increasing in volume.

Freddie climbed onto the bed behind Connor

and Ruby, who exchanged terrified looks. He put his hands on their shoulders to try to calm them, but his words were lost in the growing cacophony. Now a whirling wind picked up around them. Their hair started flying about and the computer shook on the table, as pens and pencils rolled around and toppled onto the floor.

"Keep hold of the bags, whatever you do!" shouted Freddie.

A second electrical bolt shot from the map to the door. Neptune turned his head and looked at them. He was still blowing ships, but now they could feel the cold blast of his breath in the bedroom. He winked at them and increased the pressure.

Freddie glanced at Ruby as she realised Freddie's *'stuff'* was quite possibly real. She looked crazy with excitement.

"What about my mum? I've got to be back by five o'clock," she shouted. "You weren't making it up. This is *really* happening!"

Connor was staring straight ahead. He was as excited as he had ever been, but also utterly terrified. He felt a little safer facing the vortex again and was determined not to let Freddie down. He just wanted to make it through this time.

Freddie watched the map start to pucker and warp. The pulsing lights reached a crescendo and he expected it to open any second.

All of a sudden the bedroom door burst open. Jasper and Kelvin stood in the doorway looking totally bewildered. Jasper raised his phone to take a photo as Neptune drew a great lungful of air, sucking Jasper and Kelvin into the room. Then the god of the sea blew out again, thrusting the gatecrashers into the gathering tornado of rotating objects and at the same time closing the door.

Freddie couldn't believe his eyes. Where had Jasper and Kelvin come from? This was a total nightmare. What could he do? They would all be whisked away into the tunnel any second and he certainly didn't want those two with him in Egypt. The uninvited guests were terrified and screamed for help. They were being flung around the room at increasing speed, completely out of control.

Standing in the calm centre of the storm, Freddie had an idea. He caught hold of the rope and grabbed Kelvin's leg on his next circuit. His two friends instinctively seemed to know what he was trying to do and managed to tie the end above Kelvin's ankle. Then they stopped Jasper rotating and held him above their heads. Freddie let go of Kelvin, who started circling the room again. As he had the rope attached, he completely ensnared Jasper. Then Connor and Ruby caught Kelvin and let Jasper go. He continued revolving round the room and completely tied up his small accomplice.

The two infiltrators were bound together so tightly that their screaming faces were squashed together. Freddie quickly knotted the rope and pushed them back into the maelstrom. Every time they passed Neptune he blew an icy blast at them. Gradually they froze into one solid mass of boys, rope and other debris caught up in a growing iceberg. They finally collapsed against Freddie's wardrobe, completely incapacitated.

Ruby was laughing and shouting something at the top of her voice as a huge cracking noise signalled the opening of the map. A new level of wind swirled about the room. The three of them shared a look of wonder and Freddie made a thumbs-up sign. The crack surged up the Nile just like before. Through the widening gap, they could now see the deep, rich purple colours of the vortex.

"Where's my bedroom gone?" shouted Ruby.

Connor prayed he wouldn't get stuck, and Freddie made sure the scarab was safe on the string around his neck. All three held each other tightly and when the hole was wide enough, first Connor, then Ruby and lastly Freddie flew like bullets towards the wall.

Chapter 20

The sound of the map finally splitting wide open was like every window in the world being smashed at once. By the time Freddie hurtled into the vortex, he could see Connor and Ruby ahead of him, spinning wildly out of control and bouncing off the walls. He looked back to check Jasper and Kelvin weren't able to follow. He saw the bedroom door pushed open again, and thought he saw a dark figure squeeze into the room, but the gap in the wall was closing fast and Freddie was whisked away.

He soon caught up with the others and was able to stop Ruby spinning and Connor turning end over end. Portals rushed past on either side, but Freddie was only interested in looking after his friends. Ruby screamed with delight as though she were riding a roller coaster at a theme park. As they passed the scene in Paris, Connor grasped hold of Freddie's arm in the chaos, and watched the French Revolution fly by with wonder in his eyes.

Freddie had told them about the hooded spirits in the tunnel, but nothing could quite prepare anyone for their actual appearance. It was weird enough having words, numbers, names and dates, flying around and through them, without the addition of these cloaked figures that flitted around like ghostly fish.

Freddie worked his way to the centre of the trio and they sped on in a more stable formation. Now they were able to take in the destinations that the portals offered, accompanied by the constant mash of music, voices and the rush of the vortex.

To Connor it was all as Freddie had described. He felt as if he knew every metre of the tunnel and every option the portals presented. But new portals seemed to have emerged, including the pitch-black vista of space, illuminated by a craft burning up on approach to a distant planet. He didn't like the ghostly grey figures though. They were freaky and disconcerting. Almost immediately, Connor was buffeted by one, surging ahead of the three friends. Once again they became unstable, and had to separate to avoid injuring each other. At the same time, a rush of wind from ahead slowed them until they came to an exhausted halt by the Egyptian portal.

Freddie recoiled at the sight of it. The portal now

seemed to be split in two, with a central vertical dividing line. It was night on both sides. Freddie pointed to the faint outline of the giant pyramid in the right section of the portal. *Why was it split? Could it be two Egyptian portals using the same opening? Must be,* Freddie thought. He tried to anticipate the spinning time code, waiting for 1328 BC to appear. He had a tight grip on his friends and bent down ready to pounce like a big cat at the right moment, as the hooded grey figures fussed about them.

Then, from nowhere, the dark, hooded figure reappeared and tore Ruby and Connor away from Freddie, pushing them to the right and holding Freddie at arm's length to the left. It made a grab at Freddie's neck for the scarab, but Freddie deflected the arm. The apparition shouted a torrent of abuse and, cackling with laughter, shoved Freddie, Connor and Ruby with all his might. They three entered the split Egyptian portal at the same time, but in two different places – hundreds of kilometres apart. The last thing Freddie heard as he tumbled alone through the left-hand side of the portal was the apparition's fading laughter.

Freddie was back where he began. He lay sprawled amongst the lush wet grass on the west bank of the Nile at Waset. Whereas Ruby and Connor must now be by the sphinx in Giza. He swallowed hard. This was a disaster. And the problems with their entrance had severely delayed their arrival. Freddie turned to see the date 1125 BC set, fade and then disappear. Two hundred and three years had elapsed since Freddie's first visit. Kha and Ankha would be long dead by now and the boy king would not have had his scarab to look after him on his journey. Freddie was totally distraught.

As he stood in the chill of the Egyptian dawn, he took a moment to mourn Kha and his wife. They were two beautiful souls and true friends, and he would never, ever, see them again. But he had made a promise to Ankha, and Freddie Malone always kept his promises. He couldn't risk stepping back through the portal now for fear of the dark, hooded figure. He might get involved in a battle and not be able to return the scarab at all, and also he wouldn't be in a position to rescue Ruby and Connor. For the moment at least, he had to stay this side of the portal, where at least he was in the same time zone as his two friends. *Calm down, think! One thing at a time. Oh no! My rucksack!*

His notes, calculations, torches, maps and Ankha's necklace – Connor and Ruby had everything. How much could he do from memory? He had to get to the rocky outcrop and come up with a plan. He was worried about his friends. How would they be getting on? It was difficult enough thinking for himself in these situations, let alone two novice time-travellers.

In the gathering light of dawn, he climbed quickly, watching the sunrise pierce the eastern horizon and cast its warmth over another ordinary day for Egyptians in 1125 BC.

But not quite such an ordinary day for Freddie Malone.

Meanwhile, Connor and Ruby were doing something remarkably similar. On emerging from the portal at the tail of the sphinx, Connor realised Freddie had not made it through and thought he was going to pass out. He had to be with Freddie. At no point in any planning had they thought they could be separated by some kind of evil demon in the vortex. He could not do this alone. No way! He spun round in a panic and tried to re-enter the fading portal, only for Ruby to pull him back. She put her face close to his and spoke with urgency and authority.

"Connor, listen. LISTEN! Freddie will find us. He knows where we are. Just wait here a few minutes to see if he comes. If he doesn't we'll hide above the temple and wait for him there."

Connor looked into her brilliant eyes and took a few deep breaths.

But Freddie didn't emerge.

So the pair carefully hid high above the temple altar. Connor changed into his white PE kit behind a large statue and then crawled back to join Ruby.

"There are some white robes in that side bit over there. I'm going to get one. I'll be back in a minute,"

Ruby told him.

Connor nodded and whispered, "What actually happened back there? I was too busy trying to see what was in the portal."

Ruby shrugged. "The hooded man, the bloke who probably followed Freddie round Egypt last time, pushed us through. I bet he pushed Freddie in through the other side at the same time, which means he's back in the Valley of the Kings. So at least he can return the scarab."

"*If* he had his notes to help him find the tomb," Connor said, holding up Freddie's rucksack alongside his own.

"Oh no. That's a disaster. But at least he's got the scarab."

Connor nodded and narrowed his eyes. "But how come Jasper and Kelvin were in the house? The doors were locked. How did they...?"

"What?" Ruby said defensively. "What? Why are you looking at me like that? *What?*"

"I saw you with Kelvin by the park this morning. And then all of a sudden Kelvin and Jasper turn up, just as the vortex opened. That's a bit of a coincidence, isn't it?"

Connor stared Ruby down. It was time to have it out. She looked rattled and upset, but obviously couldn't argue back too loudly for fear of them being overheard. Instead the two continued in vicious whispers.

"Were you spying on me, then?"

"No, I was in a shop and I saw you. You and Kelvin, on the pavement."

"So what?"

"I saw you. He offered you chocolate."

"So? You're not the only one who's allowed chocolate. Anyway, I didn't take it."

"That's not the point. You were talking and laughing with Kelvin, and then suddenly he's in Freddie's bedroom. What are you – a double agent?"

"You'd better take that back, buddy."

"Why? Tell me why I should. It looked suspicious to me."

Connor felt like they were two fighting cats with their backs arched and their eyes glaring.

Ruby paused and looked down. Then she spoke in a sad whisper.

"I can't believe you said that, after I stood up for you in the library. I just can't. You ungrateful... If you must know – not that it's any business of yours – that slug Kelvin asked me out. He wanted to take me to the cinema. I said no, and so he asked me again, and I said no again and he tried to get me to change my mind by giving me some chocolate, and I said no a third time and I left him to meet up with you two." She shook her head and looked away. "I thought you'd been a bit funny with me."

Connor felt completely wrong-footed. He hadn't thought of this option at all. He'd automatically thought the worst of Ruby without finding out the truth first. *Or was it the truth?* He felt like screaming.

"So how did they get into Freddie's house?" he asked.

"I don't know. I haven't got keys to Freddie's house. I only moved in two days ago! I can't believe you think I'd steal them and give them to that bunch of idiots."

"I'm sorry! That's what it looked like. You can see that."

Ruby hugged herself and turned away.

"You can look after yourself now. I'm going to wait for the vortex to open and get away from you. I really can't believe you, Connor." With that, she crawled along the beam to the edge of the wall and dropped out of sight.

Connor leaned against the base of the statue on top of the temple, staring at the great sphinx in 1125 BC. He seemed to have got things badly wrong. He didn't think he'd ever felt this lonely in his life.

Chapter 21

Freddie surveyed the changes in Waset. Looking to the west in front of the peak of Ta Dehent, the line of huge buildings on Temple Street had increased by five, each a dramatic and grand architectural giant. It was like a road in Britain with ten cathedrals side by side.

Looking back to the river, he realised something. The water level was much higher. In front of him, the banks were breached and the Nile was spreading. The season of Akhet – the Inundation – had started.

Two large ferries erratically crossed the fast-flowing water and unloaded about thirty men from each with their families. They began an orderly walk away from the river towards the workers' village of Pa Demi.

This was Freddie's chance. He didn't know *what* to do, but he knew he must do something. Sitting on a rock feeling sorry for himself was not going to solve any problems. As he climbed down, he noticed that the huge two-headed palm tree was now leaning, lifeless and leafless, against the rock. It looked like a catapult cast aside by an ogre.

He skirted the arena, joined the road and soon saw the line of workers. They were escorted by a handful of soldiers on either side.

At a rest stop, unseen by the guards, a slight young man darted away at right angles and hid behind a wall. Only Freddie saw this quick and daring move, and as the march continued, he drew level with the man, who pleaded with Freddie to remain silent.

"Why are you hiding?" Freddie uttered in his best Egyptian.

The scrawny young man with a patchy beard and huge, pleading eyes said, "Please don't give me away. I am a scribe. I have been forced to join the workforce, to dig the tomb of Ramesses."

"Why don't you want to do that?"

"Because that's where I will end my days. If you know the secrets of a tomb, you can never leave. I have a wife and child in Abdju. Because I can write, they took me and forced me to come. I need to escape."

Freddie nodded sympathetically. "I won't give you away, don't worry. But why didn't they come with you? Other men have their families here."

"My wife is expecting another child and is too ill to travel."

"What's your name?" asked Freddie, an idea forming.

The man backed away, suddenly suspicious.

"Why do you want to know?"

"Because I need a job. I need to escape my cruel uncle... Patri— err, *Hotep*. I will be safe in the village."

"But you will never be free. You will live and die there."

"I need to disappear." Freddie was doing his utmost to calm the man and looked him sincerely in the eyes.

"Intef," the man said at last. "Intef is my name. We should swap. You can be Intef and I will be...?"

"Freddie!" Intef looked understandably perplexed. "It's a foreign name, from Albanicus, far away over the sea." Freddie pointed in what he thought might be the general direction of Britain.

"Freddie! Fre-ddie! I like it. So will my wife. We shall name our next child after you in thanks. But what if it's a girl?"

"Then Ruby. Roo-bee. That's a good name."

The man rolled the words around his mouth and smiled. "You will need these."

Intef handed Freddie a reed bag with all the tools of his trade: papyrus sheets, thick and thin brushes, inking sticks, a mixing palette and several compacted, coloured mineral blocks. Freddie thanked him and shouldered the bag.

"Quickly, before I am missed," said Intef. "I will name

my children after you. And my children's children." Then he vanished into a nearby irrigation channel.

Freddie took a deep breath and hoped he was doing the right thing. He soon caught the back of the line. It was clear that the men did not know each other and that they had been recruited from many places and nationalities with the promise of a better life constructing the resting place of kings. All had uprooted their families in the pursuit of shelter, work and wealth. They looked around nervously, whispering in a dozen languages, hoping to find a countryman who understood.

The group entered the ordered settlement of the worker's village at Pa Demi. It had grown since Freddie had walked past it two hundred years before.

A rotund and smiling overseer addressed them. "Welcome to Set Ma'at – the place of truth." His heavy jowls quivered as he talked. "Those who work with their left hands, stand still. Those who work with their right hands, come over here." It was not quite a half and half split, but not far off. "I am Neferhotep," the man continued. "You will work on the greatest project of our age. You will finish the tomb of Ramesses IX. You will work hard, or die trying."

Freddie realised the smile had left the face of the large man and a rather unnerving, glazed expression had replaced it.

"In return you will be well fed and well remembered

by the gods. You have the satisfaction that although you will never leave, you will provide for your families and they will have a better life. Those of the right, join the right-hand gang in the houses behind you. Those left-handed men, follow Bek, here. You must know that the right-hand men are ahead. The left hand must catch up as there is a forfeit to pay if you don't. I'll leave you to imagine what that punishment is." The overseer, Neferhotep, returned to the meal he had been disturbed from, but added, "Where are the scribes I sent for?"

A tall, painfully thin young man reluctantly stepped forward and Freddie, realising it was his cue, did the same.

"Yes, I can see why you're scribes." Neferhotep laughed at his own joke, supported by Bek, who despite being small, was comprised entirely of muscle and gave off a fizzing, dangerous energy. "You two little flowers have got it easy. You just have to record the work, the hours, the absentees and the progress. Your reports will be sent to our glorious pharaoh. But remember I can read, so don't try sending him any personal messages, or I will feed you to Bek here. Do you understand?"

"Yes, sir. I understand," Freddie replied.

"I didn't ask for a conversation!" sneered the huge man, as he ripped some meat away from a bone and dipped it in a thick, brown sauce. Chewing noisily, he waved a chubby hand to dismiss the gathering.

Bek led the left-handed men to the densely packed, single-storey, flat-roofed mud houses on the left-hand side of the main street. Each house contained up to twenty people, who shared a kitchen, living room, courtyard and cellar. There were about seventy houses, including those of the right-hand gang and Freddie was allocated a room with three other men already there. He found a sleeping space and inherited a rancid old reed mat. The only good thing was that it was close to the stairs that led up to the flat roof.

He was greeted with absolute indifference by two of the men, who spoke little Egyptian. The final occupant was a very frail, elderly man who seemed to have trouble breathing.

"So you're the new scribe?" the old man's shaky voice enquired, as Freddie carefully examined his new work tools.

"Yes, yes I am, although I'm not very experienced. My name is Fr— err, *Intef!* I'm from Albanicus. Are you a scribe too?"

"Yes, I am Ani, the oldest man in this hellhole. I have worked here for many years, and on many tombs. You are my replacement. I can no longer work. I think my time is short." Freddie fetched Ani some water from a large stone jug in the tiny kitchen space and helped the old man to drink. He was virtually skin and bone and smiled his thanks to Freddie.

"I don't envy you, Intef – this is a time of great unrest. You new men are here because we had a strike, then a riot, and many men were taken away. We won't see them again, or their families. This used to be such a noble place to work. It is a great craft to build a tomb, but now they just want it done faster and cheaper. I wait for the great god Amun to call me to the other side," – he laughed – "but I don't really believe in all that. If it does exist, the kingdom of Osiris must be very, very crowded." He laughed again and a weak, chesty rattle seemed to exhaust him. "Tell me of your country. The only places I have ever seen are the temple sites over the water and this dark underground existence."

Freddie spent a long time talking about Albanicus, 'The Green Land of Rain', as he described it. Later, as the afternoon wore on, the old scribe helped Freddie with the skills he would need.

"The overseer will dictate what you write, except for the daily measurements. You'll be with the left-hand gang, but always record what the right-hand has done as well. The left and right gangs work separately so they don't get in each other's way.

"Pray you avoid flint in the limestone. Flint is the enemy. It will halt your progress. Keep your team supplied with light. Make sure the linen wicks of the torches are soaked in oil and grease. But you must add salt to stop them smoking. Don't ask me how it works, it just does. It's underground magic. Spend two days a week preparing your papyrus. One to strip and plait the reeds and soak them. The second to paste the linen on and dry them flat on the roof. Most importantly, write small. The larger you write, the more papyrus you'll need." He laughed and coughed again.

Freddie practised his lettering and hieroglyphics until his new mentor was satisfied.

"You will be fine. You are a strong boy who will become an even stronger man. I must sleep now." He turned on his matting to get more comfortable. In seconds he was asleep and oblivious to the horn that assembled the left-hand gang.

Outside, Bek counted them. "Thirty-seven. Five less than the right-hand. You are already behind so you will have to work twice as hard to catch up."

With that motivational speech ringing in their ears, they set off for the East Valley along the workers' path. They passed the right-hand gang, marching back after their shift. Jokes and boasts were shared between the two sets of men.

In the dwindling light, Freddie could see that nothing much had changed. There was no sign of tomb 62. Kha's burial place was completely hidden. It looked like a group of three workshops stood roughly where the entrance might be, but it was impossible to tell. Not even the entrance to the tomb of Ramesses VI could be seen, built in the hillside immediately over

Kha's tomb. Every way in was disguised and hidden. The rough scree slopes camouflaged everything.

The inside of Ramesses IX's tomb was huge. Past the pillared hall a steep slope led to the burial chamber, which was in the process of excavation. When it was finished, it would be 170 metres from the valley entrance to the back wall.

The sounds of chisels attacking the stubborn stone continued through the night, and as daylight broke, the workers set off back over the hill. Almost immediately the line of the returning right-hand gang snaked towards them and the jokers lifted their voices once more.

And so the routine went on. Shift followed shift, but still Freddie had no idea where Kha was buried.

After a week, through hard work and camaraderie, the left-hand gang caught up and overtook the right, who had hit flint.

Freddie checked his records every morning with Ani and after sleeping, and when Ani felt well enough to climb the steps, they spent hours together chatting as they plaited new papyrus on the roof. But as he listened to the old scribe, Freddie was often preoccupied by thoughts of what could be happening to Connor and Ruby. He hoped beyond hope that they were safe.

Freddie was always helpful around the village, and was adopted by a kind, matronly Hittite woman called Henti, who spoiled him with food in return for his patient play with her two grandsons. They played catch with clay balls full of rattling seeds, and they hit sticks, mastering the game tip-cat. They spent time playing *Mehen*, the snake game, where the winner was the first to move their counter around the squares of a carved stone to the centre. Freddie's patience was inexhaustible.

But there was always an undercurrent of bad feeling in the camp, and arguments sparked easily. Fights broke out. Things came to a head when their food rations were halved and the workers' families all became ill from foul water.

A stand-off with Bek and Neferhotep only resulted in the ringleader being led away and never seen again. This ended the revolt, but it didn't stop the hatred and resentment escalating.

It was during his eighth long shift underground that Freddie was sent to the storeroom, near where he thought Kha's tomb had to be hidden. But without his notebook and measurements, he was lost. He couldn't just start digging.

Once he had gathered the spare torches needed, he looked quickly in the adjoining workshops. In the largest, stonemasons carved decorative pieces whilst sheltering from the sun. A shadoof had been adapted to lift stone away from a large raised work slab. Freddie could see no sign of the rubbish pit that covered the pipe tunnel. He made his mind up. He had to get back through the portal and find Connor and Ruby, then bring them back here. *Yeah, good luck with that!* he heard his Uncle Patrick's voice in his head. *Easier said than done.*

Freddie had to escape and it had to be at night. He needed to disappear as the gang set off for work tomorrow evening. They were guarded as they walked, but only by three or four bored, elderly soldiers. So he knew *when* he was going to do it, but he would leave *how* until the moment arose. Any plan he made now was bound to be different on the day.

As the left-hand gang returned home, they passed a group of women carrying a shrouded body, heading for the burial vault in the nearby hillside. Freddie's senses tingled. He knew what had happened. Ani was nowhere to be found. Henti entered, wiping tears from her eyes before sifting through the old man's belongings. She found nothing she wanted and handed some fine paintbrushes to Freddie. He added them to Intef's collection and helped clear the space, ready for whoever came next. He hadn't even said goodbye to Ani. When he'd gone to work, the kind old man had been dozing.

After Henti left, he finished clearing the space and dislodged a stone in the wall, behind which were hidden seven medals. One for each of the tombs Ani had worked on in his lifetime. Freddie studied them and rubbed them clean. He decided to take them as they could well come in useful and they were certainly no use to Ani anymore.

Freddie was extremely saddened by his friend's death and fell restlessly asleep. He awoke hours later to see the empty space at his side, and his restless mind full of thoughts of Connor and Ruby. He had to get to them as soon as he could.

He had a strong feeling he was desperately needed in Giza.

Chapter 22

A long, long way north, Connor wept a constant stream of salty tears. His usually neat appearance was spoiled by the sweat that caked his hair to his scalp, and the heat that turned his complexion crimson. He felt entirely miserable. His body shuddered as another wave of grief and self-pity overtook him. The adventure wasn't meant to be like this at all. His eyes squinted against the bright sunlight, as he scanned the surroundings hoping to catch a glimpse of his friend. He hadn't meant to upset Ruby, but he'd been entitled to question her, surely? Her behaviour *had* looked suspicious.

Connor hid the rucksacks behind the statue's base and he stayed in the shade that it cast. It was some time since Ruby had disappeared and he was desperate for her to return so he could say sorry properly.

But what if he *was* right? His mind still flipped between the two possibilities.

There was only one course of action – the immediate consumption of anything chocolatey. But even that brief feast didn't solve anything.

In the early morning light, merchants started appearing from all directions and erected shady awnings in the large space in front of Connor to the left of the sphinx and in front of the central pyramid. Before long, a makeshift market had appeared from nowhere.

How was he going to explain all this to his best friend? Freddie would never trust him again. Somehow he had to rescue the situation and make amends for his mistake. And what would they say to Ruby's mum? *Sorry, she's stuck in 1125 bc. She might be back in a year or two!*

Connor began to apply sun cream liberally. He had already started burning and the heat was murderous for a boy of his size. From somewhere behind him a vicious crack of a whip and violent shouts split the air. Around the corner of the temple appeared a sorry gaggle of heavily shackled slaves tied together by their right legs. With their heads bowed and their hands bound behind their backs, they each echoed the movements of the captive in front of them. They had no choice. In this way, just a handful of slave drivers were able to march thirty men, women and children towards the central space of the market.

Connor felt immense pity for the captives. His eyes trailed over each sorry figure. Then his heart almost stopped when he saw who was being dragged along at the back of the line. Ruby! She looked desperately round to the temple roof, but stumbled before she saw Connor wave at her. She was hauled upright by a small, shouting man who threatened to hit her.

A fresh wave of anguish flooded through Connor. "Oh no! What have I done?" he whispered in a horrified gasp. This was a disaster. If only he'd kept his mouth shut!

The slaves were made to squat in the dust. The biggest slave driver walked among them, shouting an indistinct rant. When his back was turned, two women ran with a jug and gave small sips of water to the slaves at the end of the line, before the brute frightened them off. At least Ruby was one of the lucky ones who'd had a mouthful of water.

Connor was completely numb with shock. He needed a plan and he needed it fast. Pulling himself together he recovered the notebook, the multi-tool and precious necklace from Freddie's rucksack. He crammed everything into the pockets of his shorts.

A crowd gathered for the auction. It was now or never. He carefully climbed down and crept into the temple. He hid behind a large pillar and when the coast was clear, like Ruby, he took one of the white robes. He covered himself roughly and plunged into the market, looking rather like a melting snowman.

By the time Connor arrived breathlessly at the auction, two slaves had already been sold and the brute was pitching to the crowd with a well-practised patter. One guard sat cross-legged at the end of the line next to Ruby. Connor thought about how he could create a distraction so he could try and free her. *What would Freddie do? Think!*

Buyers inspected the slaves. A huge captive man who had double the rope restraints of the others sat three in front of Ruby. He was constantly being made to stand and show his teeth to potential owners. After the fifth time, he bellowed his anger and thrashed about on his rope. The slave drivers rushed to control his dangerous outburst. Three of them ended up hanging off the man, as he swung them about like rag dolls.

Connor seized his chance and ran to Ruby. Her bright blue eyes shot open in shock, then gratitude. He started hacking lumps out of the rough hemp rope with the multi-tool's knife attachment.

"Hurry up!" Ruby pleaded. "Just do my feet, then we can get out of here."

"I'm trying. It's really thick!" Sweat streamed into Connor's eyes.

The disturbance along the line continued, and the curious crowd competed to catch a glimpse of the furious giant. Connor frantically cut at the rope.

"I'm nearly through. Get ready to run."

"I'm ready."

The last few obstinate strands gave way and Connor jumped up, feeling light-headed after the extreme effort. He tried to pull Ruby away, but for some reason she didn't move. Connor blinked and now saw that Ruby was firmly held by the large slave driver and already in the process of being retied.

Connor skilfully pocketed the multi-tool before his hands were roughly pulled behind him. Then he and Ruby were circled in rope, back-to-back and shoved to the ground.

"I'm really sorry, Ruby," spluttered Connor, shaking his head in hopeless frustration. "I bet Freddie would have rescued you. I'm just—"

"Don't worry, bud. You tried. We nearly got away. You did brilliantly." Ruby's tone was soothing. Connor searched for the knots around her wrists but couldn't find them. She did the same. No luck.

"I'm sorry I doubted you about Kelvin. I should have said something straight away. I really am dead sorry." Connor felt his shoulders start to shake.

"Don't wimp out on me now, Conman. I could have told you both, but I thought it would look like I was boasting. I'm not used to boys asking me out. I'm more used to them laughing and running away."

"That's mad, you're brilliant. The sort of boys that do that aren't worth your time. They're idiots."

"Thanks, buddy. But, err – changing the subject

slightly. We're tied up together in a market in ancient Egypt, about to be sold as slaves. What do we do now? We've got to come up with a plan. And quickly!"

Connor needed to reassure her. "Freddie will be looking for us. I bet he's on his way up the river now. He's probably stowed away on another boat."

"Yeah, he'll come straight here. He knows we arrived at the sphinx," Ruby continued, optimistically. Connor wished he believed even half of this, but he felt he was helping Ruby by being positive.

Being bound together made Connor think of Jasper and Kelvin tied up in Freddie's bedroom. He really wished he and Ruby could change places with them.

"I'm sorry, Ruby, I'll never doubt you again."

"It's OK, we'll get over it, no problemo!" She paused, then suddenly spoke in a small voice. "Connor, I really don't want to be a slave. Can't you find the knots? We've got to escape now."

The huge captive, standing tall and staring into the far distance, had triggered a four-way bidding war. When sold, he fetched a massive price and the excited crowd started to disperse, leaving the traders eagerly inspecting the jewellery and precious stones they'd finally accepted for him.

By the time Connor and Ruby were hauled to their feet for sale, it seemed like no one could care less. Ruby attracted a little interest but refused to show her teeth. Even when forced, she bit the hand of the only prospective purchaser. The small trader reacted furiously and tried to hit her, but Connor turned at the last second and bravely took the glancing slap. The men laughed. They clearly just wanted to sell these last two and be done.

"Stick to the plan," Connor whispered, a fat lip already growing from the blow. The laughing traders joked amongst themselves, gesticulating wildly about Connor's size. It appeared no one would be interested in a slave who looked like he would eat them out of house and home. Ruby found his fingers and squeezed them supportively. He whispered his thanks. She didn't let go and the comfort flooded through them both.

Friends again.

Chapter 23

Suddenly a commotion from the direction of the temple caught everyone's attention. An elderly sandy-haired man ran towards them. His arms and legs shot out at all angles. He was frantically waving at the traders and shouting in a weedy, high-pitched voice. He arrived as a clown might in a circus ring, skidding in the dust. It appeared he needed slaves and the traders pointed to their last two offerings. The man stamped his foot and voiced his disgust at the disappointing prospect of Ruby and Connor.

The rope binding them together was untied, so they stood side by side. Instead of wanting to look at their teeth, the strange old man stuck his tongue out. Ruby refused. He repeated the action to Connor, but recoiled slightly at the sight that greeted him.

The eccentric old man pulled at his wispy beard

and asked a price, which the brutish slaver gruffly gave. The man's pointed features creased with laughter and he walked away.

The slaver shouted a second option. The man stopped in his tracks, turned, tilted his head and replied with a counter offer. The slavers snorted in contempt, but on inspection of the two bracelets on offer, they eventually gave a third price. The willowy man scratched his chin, then slowly disentangled a further small loop of dull beads. Connor watched, aghast. Could the adventure have gone any worse, than being sold as slaves for three paltry wristbands? But there was one good thing.

"At least we're together," Ruby said.

"I know," he replied.

The price was obviously less than the slavers wanted, but they'd had enough for today. They took their ropes and were gone.

But Ruby and Connor still had their hands tied and now the sandy-haired man produced a fine, multicoloured, flat string and wound it around both their necks. It was a fragile, gossamer tether that looked as if it would break easily, but it was sharp at the edges and incredibly strong. The eccentric old man simply pressed the string together and it bonded instantly, as if it had a coating of superglue. It was immovable. Connor's mouth gaped open as the man smiled with undisguised delight. This had to be something magical.

"Wow, cool!" Ruby said.

The man pulled them along behind him. They had to follow swiftly or the string cut into their necks. It sparkled in the fierce sunlight and its rainbow of coloured threads contrasted with the barren desert that surrounded them on all sides.

"This is like barbed wire. It keeps nipping my neck," complained Ruby.

"Just walk smoothly, keep your head level. We'll find a way to escape soon." They whispered hopeless escape plans to each other as they were led like mules.

After an hour, they reached a busy village still within sight of the pyramids and were led through a courtyard into a small, dark shop. Connor gazed about at the hundreds of coloured clay and glass bottles that lined tightly packed shelves on all sides. Mixing bowls, dried plants, candles and scales were set out on a central table, with some chairs scattered nearby and a fire pit in one corner.

"What's going on here?" Ruby said.

The man pointed to himself and said weedily, "Timna." He repeated this two or three times, tapping his chest. Seeing him close up was a shock. His face was criss-crossed with deep lines and he was obviously incredibly old, yet he was surprisingly agile and sprightly. There was definitely something very unusual about him, which Connor couldn't quite put his finger on.

He led his new servants to a post by the fire pit and

looped the loose end of the string around it. Again, he simply touched the string together lightly between his fingers, creating an instant and incredibly strong seal.

Timna was talking excitedly, seemingly asking them questions, which were of course completely incomprehensible to Ruby and Connor. But it didn't seem to bother him that they couldn't answer. He clapped his hands and jigged round the room, stopping by the far wall where, from a low shelf, he took a sip from each of six coloured bottles and two larger swigs from a seventh.

"He's on drugs!" Connor whispered.

"He's bonkers," Ruby added.

Customers had formed a patient queue outside. Timna began serving, selling his concoctions with an entertaining charm. His new servants stood bewildered, swapping nervous glances. Connor wondered at Ruby. She seemed to be finding it all fascinating, and her lack of anxiety about their predicament was the only thing that kept him going.

Then, one old lady in the queue caught their eyes and drew a finger across her throat like a pantomime pirate. Seeing this made Connor whimper and go weak at the knees.

"Hold it together, Connor. Be strong, buddy. She's just winding us up."

After the last customer was served, Timna took a small red bottle from the left-hand pocket of his shendyt, went over to the post they were tethered to and poured a drop of liquid. In an instant, the knot in the rainbow string dissolved.

"OK, so he's properly a wizard," Ruby breathed.

Timna then led Ruby and Connor outside and reshackled them to a shady tree with another simple touch. It was like a magical, immovable Velcro. Timna pointed to Ruby and then to the food, pots and clay oven, then with the use of an extravagant mime, indicated that she should produce a feast.

"Why hasn't he got you doing the cooking?" she huffed to Connor. Ruby grumpily turned herself to the task. She put meat and vegetables in a metal pan over the flames and moved them about a bit. From a distance Connor offered helpful advice. Ruby gratefully accepted, grumbling to herself about sexism and stereotypes.

Connor was ordered by Timna to shift a huge pile of heavy sacks, full of foul-smelling dried herbs and animal bones, from outside into the shop. After moving ten sacks, he was exhausted. Timna shook his head and swapped his slaves, so Ruby carried the sacks and Connor bent low over the fire to complete supper. By the time the food was cooked, Connor's face, already red, had darkened to purple with the effort and the heat.

Ruby shifted the remaining sacks in the time it had taken Connor to move two and Timna's foul mood lifted.

He directed Ruby to bring all the sacks from the shop into a large adjacent private room. This was Timna's workshop, where he was creating a large quantity of a light-blue potion in a big cauldron. Papyruses and diagrams were scattered everywhere, detailing his recipes. Only one wall had shelves, but there were at least ten of them rising every 30 centimetres or so right up to the ceiling.

Whilst Ruby shuffled backwards and forwards with the sacks, Timna used a ladder to stock his shelves with the latest batches. Hundreds of brightly coloured bottles lined the wall in groups of twenty or so, except for the top shelf, that only had dark-blue and the new light-blue bottles on it. This room was also where Timna slept, as there was a reed mat and scattered clothes along the opposite wall from the shelves. It was as if he didn't like straying too far from his precious medicines. There was a folding screen at the far end of the room which Ruby couldn't see behind.

Eventually, darkness fell and Timna demanded his food. He sat expectantly at a table under the stars. Connor, quite proudly, presented the meat and vegetables along with bread and fruit, and Timna cautiously began to eat. He was transfixed. The flavours were perfect and he made little happy eating noises like they do on cookery programmes. He also did a mime that roughly translated as, *I can understand why you're so fat.* What was left was shared between

Ruby and a sweaty and relieved chef. Connor gave her a bigger portion as he'd sampled masses as it was cooking. Ruby looked across at Connor in amazement.

"How come, buddy? Who knew?"

"I got the recipes in the library, remember? And I watch all those chefs on TV. You've got to be bold with your flavours, it's about getting the spices right, that's the trick." Connor blushed with pride.

"It's fantastic, buddy. Brilliant! Listen, we've got to talk. When he goes to sleep we'll catch up." Connor nodded.

Timna pointed to an outhouse with straw on the floor and retied his servants inside on a very short leash. Luckily a bright moon gave plenty of light through the door and window and when they were convinced Timna was asleep, Connor proudly produced Freddie's notebook, multi-tool and the necklace. He smiled at Ruby and raised an eyebrow like James Bond.

"You genius, Connor. You absolute legend," beamed Ruby. "Now let's plan."

Chapter 24

They quickly established that even the multi-tool couldn't cut the magical string.

"I can't believe it," uttered a deflated Connor.

"We need that red bottle from his pocket," Ruby said. Using the vocabulary in Freddie's notes, she worked out that the orange bottles contained a sleeping potion, because a lady had bought two more, praising Timna for her first good night in years.

By testing each other constantly on all the Egyptian words Freddie had listed, they soon understood scraps of Timna's conversations. A shop is always a haven for gossip and Timna also had a very handy habit of talking out loud to himself when alone, providing a great additional source of information.

A man came in on their second day asking about his new slaves as the old ones had only worked at the shop a short while before disappearing. Timna was instantly defensive and brushed the questions aside, instead producing a sticky brown paste, which he said would cure the man's baldness. Timna was a master salesman and the man left with expensive hair gel and none of his questions answered.

Timna turned to his neatly lined bottles and talked to them like children, "Test… slaves…" Timna cackled and obviously felt safe spouting in Egyptian, thinking that Ruby and Connor were none the wiser.

"Test? Slaves!" said Connor. "That doesn't sound good." His face betrayed his fears and he added, "Don't let him give you anything to eat or drink from his bottles."

"It's all right for you, he thinks you're brilliant. He's got guests coming tomorrow to taste your food. He's not going risk losing you, buddy. I'm the one he'll test stuff on."

"I hope not," Connor replied. Ruby looked concerned, so he added, "I'll make sure nothing happens to you. I'm just one meal away from failure. Don't worry. We'll stay safe."

Ruby nodded. "If you say so, Conman. But what's in the bottles on the top shelf? He's really secretive when he goes up there. He always checks I'm not sneaking a look," she mused. "There's two sorts of blue bottles. He takes a little swig out of a darker bottle, once in the morning, before the first customers arrive, and then again before his supper. He's always much livelier when he's drunk the potion. Must be herbs and stuff. Like a health supplement."

"I could do with a bit of that. I'm melting in this heat. Then *slaving* over a hot fire all day..." They both laughed. The situation was preposterous yet, bizarrely, Connor felt they were really enjoying themselves. He just had to glance up from his food prep to see the top of the sphinx's head and the three huge pyramids behind it. Each and every time, it took his breath away, but he wished Freddie were here to share it all.

Ruby seemed to do all the hard physical work for which she was better suited, and it gave her quite a bit more freedom. Although always attached by the coloured string, she could quite often spy on Timna without him knowing.

"I wonder how Freddie's doing," Ruby whispered, as they tried to sleep on the hard floor.

"I bet he's on his way."

Ruby pulled a face. "You and your bets! How will he find us?"

They both fell silent for a moment.

"We'll be all right. We'll get that red bottle from his pocket and release ourselves. I won't let anything bad happen to you, Ruby, I promise."

Ruby looked at Connor and thought for a long time before smiling. "I know, bud," she said. "We'll look after each other, right?"

The following evening, their fourth in Timna's service, two couples were to be entertained at supper. There was a lot of pressure on Connor to deliver a great meal. But with Timna preoccupied with guests, it might give them a chance to steal the red solvent. No matter how hard they spied on Timna, they could only see one red bottle and it stayed with him at all times.

Everything went well. Connor only lost his cool once, storming off like a temperamental TV chef because the sauce he was cooking for the beef was the wrong consistency. Well, he tried to storm off, but was stopped by a sharp tug on his neck as he reached the limit of his leash. He looked sheepishly at Ruby, who burst out laughing and gently reeled him back. He couldn't help smiling at his own stupidity, but was relieved when the sauce at last thickened to perfection.

Timna's absent-minded mutterings informed them that the main guest tonight was an army general. Hands were shaken, a deal was done and a bag of precious stones changed hands.

Connor's talents were enhancing Timna's reputation rapidly. The general wanted to meet the chef and Connor was summoned.

"Why... Tied... Dog?" he asked of Timna.

"Precious... Jewel..." the apothecary replied, patting Connor on the shoulder. Ruby cleared the table and could see that when Timna was seated, the solvent bottle stuck out of the small pouch sewn into his shendyt. Stealing it was their only chance of escape – if it could be done.

They ate well that night as Timna had insisted a huge amount of food was cooked.

"That sauce is amazing, buddy. What's in it?"

"Wine, flour, onions and… powder." Connor went quiet on the last ingredient.

"Powder? Powdered what? Go on, tell me. What powder?"

"Err… locust. Like a grasshopper, but bigger. That's what gives it the rich flavour," he added hopefully.

"Locust? Well it's brilliant, buddy, that's all I can say."

She launched into another huge mouthful, before hopping around the remnants of the fire, imitating the insect.

Every day they learned more, and every evening Timna summoned influential customers to partake of his chef's creations. He was getting a lot of respect from his important guests and Timna was taking advantage of it. He built from the first meal for five, to seven, then nine, until after a week, he announced that twelve guests were expected in two days' time. They would have to go to market to buy all the ingredients, as they were very important people. Connor blew out his cheeks.

"You can do it," Ruby told him.

"Yeah! But what shall I give them for pudding?" he replied distractedly, consulting his recipes in Freddie's notebook.

Ruby always tried to use variations in routine to search for hidden stocks of the solvent. Once, she'd even moved the ladder in Timna's room before having to return it quickly on hearing him approach.

Timna had entered with a woman customer. He was spouting a list of pharaohs. Why, Ruby had no idea, but it always started, "Kheti, Kheti, Merikara, Intef, Intef, Intef, Mentuhotep..." And he was up to "Thutmose, Thutmose, Thutmose," as the wide-eyed woman tamely nodded agreement to all the potions Timna offered. He carried on to a thunderous climax shouting, "Ramesses, Ramesses, Ramesses!" He held his hands aloft like a magician at the end of a trick. The transfixed woman parted with a fortune in precious metals, and left Timna's shop completely bamboozled. Timna laughed and jigged around jangling his easily won booty.

The daily repetition of the list of pharaohs drove Ruby mad. She needed to know why he did it and redoubled her efforts with the Egyptian vocabulary.

Later that day a seriously angry young man arrived, demanding Timna do something. A potion he'd sold yesterday had made his father dangerously sick and he waved the remnants of the light-blue medicine at the apothecary. Timna took the man inside to pacify him. Ruby crept into the shop and saw Timna exchange the light-blue for a dark-blue bottle, which Timna assured the worried customer was going to do the trick. When he'd gone, Timna poured the remnants over a potted herb and it withered instantly. Ruby was instructed to empty the stock of light-blue medicine in the dust behind the house, whilst her master began a fresh brew in the cauldron. Ruby knew she didn't want *any* of his medicine, *whatever* the colour.

On market day, they set out before dawn. Timna was determined to get the freshest ingredients possible. They were ahead of most of the merchants and waited in the shade of the sphinx while more traders arrived. Connor and Ruby looked for signs of the portal, but there were none. Connor tentatively tried reciting 'If—' but nothing happened.

"What are you doing?" hissed Ruby.

"It's Freddie's escape poem, remember?"

"Of course! Cool, you'll have to teach me."

"That's the problem. I can't quite remember all the verses," sighed Connor. "I didn't think I'd need it coz I thought Freddie would always be here."

"Ah… Tricky… well, start by calming down. I always remember stuff better when I'm not panicking. You'll do it, no probs!" said Ruby.

But try as he might, Connor couldn't remember all of the verses. So for now, they were stuck.

Timna toured the stalls looking for the best of the

best. Beautiful barbel, catfish and soft-shelled turtles caught the eye. Stunning vegetables bursting with colour. Meats, breads and figs were tested by both Timna and Connor, so that no mistakes were made, then the vital fresh spices and herbs; coriander, cumin, fennel, dill and fresh almond oil. Finally honey, yoghurt, sesame seeds and dates. A huge amount of food stood in a pile, far too much to carry.

Timna went in search of the boys who hired out handcarts and their carrying services. Ruby and Connor were left tied to a post to guard the purchases, receiving sympathetic looks from all who passed. Slavery was common, but the string round their necks was unusually demeaning. The same woman as last week stepped forward with a jug of water and gently poured it into the grateful mouths of first Ruby and then Connor, who spluttered his almost entirely into the dust as his gaze fell on three figures walking towards them.

Timna was striding slightly ahead of a stick-thin, ten-year-old boy who was pushing a cart. A bigger boy followed behind, who unswathed his facecloth to reveal a huge grinning smile.

It was Freddie!

Connor nearly shouted out to him, but stopped himself just in time and instead blinked away a few spontaneous tears of relief. Ruby erupted into a huge smile. She nudged Connor. "Act natural, buddy."

Freddie had never seen a more welcome sight than his two friends in the bustle of the market. They were alive and in one piece. He had been observing them for an hour, waiting for an opportunity to make contact. He predicted that the strange man leading Connor and Ruby about on a coloured string would need transport to deal with his stack of provisions. He spied the carters waiting in the shadow of the sphinx and recruited the smallest and hungriest-looking with the promise of one of Ani's tomb medals. His name was Menna, and as Timna approached, all the other boys, who up to this point had been very eager for work, faded into the shadows to avoid the strange-looking man. This left Menna and Freddie as the only option. Freddie breathed a sigh of relief when he realised he'd pulled it off.

Menna started loading the cart with Freddie's help, but was transfixed by Ruby's blue hair and the coloured string round the captives' necks. A moment later, the cart was full and ready for the journey. Connor and Ruby had badly disguised smiles on their faces.

Timna had attached his slaves to the cart and often marched on ahead excitedly, before stopping and letting the heavy load catch up. The three friends exchanged information in short bursts.

"Have you got the necklace, Connor?" whispered Freddie.

Connor nodded.

"Yes, it's in my pocket. I thought about wearing it, but it's not my colour... Sorry! Hello, mate."

"Hello! Yeah, sorry, hiya. Where are my manners? Fancy seeing you two here." Freddie's eyes twinkled. The three laughed as quietly as possible.

"We need you to get things for us, if you can," Ruby said, with an eye on Timna up ahead. "We need a special red bottle from his left-hand pocket. That will free us from this rope."

"Why don't you just cut it?"

Ruby rolled her eyes.

"Don't you think we've tried that, buddy? It has magical powers. It's stronger than metal, and it won't even burn. But the red bottle's got a solution in it that melts the knots. It's amazi—" Ruby went quiet as they once again caught up with the mad apothecary, who spoke harshly to the two carriers. Freddie answered back fluently, "We're doing our best, but it's heavy. We can unload it and leave it here if you're not happy."

Connor was impressed with his friend's Egyptian, and Menna smiled in wonder at Freddie's confidence. Timna huffed, but the rest of the journey passed easily, allowing them to catch up on news.

"Have you got my notebook?" Freddie asked, almost afraid to hear the answer. "That's the most important thing."

Connor whispered back. "Yes, all safe. The recipes I wrote in there have come in really handy."

"What?" asked a baffled Freddie. They quickly related the rest of the story of their week in captivity, as Freddie listened open-mouthed to their inventiveness and resilience. He shook his head in wonder.

"You two are brilliant."

"So we need to get the solvent from his shendyt pocket and we need to get a blue bottle from the top shelf in his room. And we *really* need to know why he recites a long list of pharaohs ten times a day," Ruby whispered.

Connor had a brainwave. "I've got an idea. What about that sleeping potion he gave that woman? Why don't I put that in their pudding and make them all zonk out? And then we escape."

Ruby grinned. "Brilliant, buddy!"

"Yep. Fantastic, Connor," Freddie added. Ruby explained where the sleeping potion was and how to get Timna's storeroom ladder up to reach the top shelf, where the dark-blue bottles were kept.

"Whatever you do, don't get the light-blue medicine, it gives people gut rot." Freddie nodded. "Right, I'll do all that while the feast is on."

"Great," said Ruby. "But what about you? Where have you been?"

He smiled. "I don't reckon it's nearly as exciting."

For the remainder of the walk, Freddie told them about the left-hand gang, working as a scribe in a tomb, and that without his notes, he couldn't find where Kha was buried.

"Oh no!" Connor said loudly, causing Timna to turn around. Connor made it look like things were slipping from the cart, "No, No, No!" he directed at Freddie, wagging his finger at him as if telling him off. Timna, reassured, smiled at his culinary genius and continued on.

"Phew! Sorry. So that means…"

"Yup. We've got to go back to Waset, as soon as we get a chance."

"Wow!" said Connor.

"That's incredible. I'm in!" whispered Ruby, without hesitation. Connor nodded nervously, not really sure what he wanted at that particular moment, other than cheese and onion crisps.

"Great," Freddie whispered. "Keep alert at all times. We might get a chance to escape at any moment."

The three chatted non-stop, often so quietly they had to repeat things to be understood. Menna's huge brown eyes looked from one to the other in wonder, this wasn't like his usual market day home delivery. "These are my friends," Freddie reassured him. "I have to rescue them."

"You'd better be quick," Menna replied. "This man's mad! He gets through slaves like I eat bread. No offence, but he always buys the cheap stragglers at the end of the market that no one else wants. Everyone's scared of him." Freddie didn't translate this, there was no sense worrying Ruby and Connor further right now.

As soon as they reached the apothecary's house, where a small queue of customers had formed, they put all the stores in the outhouse, out of the sun. Freddie watched with amazement as Timna's solvent loosened the invisible knot that had tied his slaves to the cart. He then lengthened their leashes so they could go about their chores. Getting that bottle was Freddie's number-one priority.

Although it was only midday, Connor had to start work for the evening's special guests. Every customer Timna served came to inspect Connor's handiwork. His recipes and reputation were spreading fast.

Menna and Freddie went into the dark shop for payment. Timna made great play of dividing a small loaf in two and gave the boys one half each. They looked at him in disgust, and Menna, finding strength from Freddie, protested that they'd been promised more. Freddie used the distraction to check the room. He spotted the sleeping potion easily enough, but how many of the orange bottles would they need to knock out thirteen people?

He could see through the doorway to the storeroom as the curtain was pulled back. The shelves were straight ahead and the blue bottles right at the top. Now all he needed was an opportunity to get to them.

"All right, all right! Here's more you thieving little..."

Freddie looked the swindling chemist right in the eye. "It's what you owe. If you don't pay, we'll load everything up and take it back."

"You wouldn't dare." Timna's wild eyes danced in defiance.

"Wouldn't we?" said Freddie returning a look that meant serious business. Timna had a queue to serve, where the profit from one customer would fund fifty cart journeys from the market. After a few seconds, and with a weedy laugh, he threw a second loaf on to the dirt floor. Menna scrambled to collect it as Freddie strode from the shop stealing a quick word with Ruby.

"It's too dangerous to hang around here this afternoon. He's bound to go into the outhouse for something. I'll go and get the rucksacks to save time later, then as soon as the light starts to fade, I'll come straight back and get what we need. Be ready to distract him. Good luck. Wow, Connor, that smells good!"

As soon as they rounded the building, Freddie pressed Menna to tell all he knew about Timna.

"Some say he kills them. I don't know. I wouldn't normally carry for him, but because you came, I felt safe."

"Why would he kill them?"

"To test his potions, that's what the other carters say. What's that coloured string all about? I hope your friends are safe."

An hour later, back at the sphinx, Freddie gave each

of the carters one of Ani's tomb medals, and to Menna he presented half the stones from Ankha's necklace. It was like having ten years' pay in one day. The wide-eyed boys were so excited they hugged each other and Freddie, and thanked him over and over again.

Menna stood mesmerised, staring at the objects which had changed his fortunes. He gently cradled the jewels like a mother would a newborn baby, before carefully placing them in his shendyt pocket. He smiled again in wonder, his eyes brimful of tears. Then after a reassuring nod from Freddie, Menna turned and walked away to a better life, thanks to Freddie Malone and the wealth of a long-dead boy king and his wonderful queen.

Chapter 25

Freddie found the rucksacks easily enough. A swarm of flies was feasting on a split packet of chocolate-covered raisins. They had festered for a week in the heat, providing a banquet for every insect in Giza. As he emptied everything out and repacked the bags, he noticed how things had disintegrated in the years since he had been here before. The harsh, unrelenting sun had roasted the stone and caused sections of the pyramids and sphinx to wear away.

Freddie set off to rescue Connor and Ruby. He was proud of the way they had coped without him, but the scarab round his neck reminded him that their mission was still incomplete.

At dusk, as he neared Timna's chaotic scattering of buildings, he saw a cluster of well-dressed guests gathered in the courtyard. Instead of Connor being hidden away cooking out of sight, he seemed instead to be the main attraction as everyone studied his methods.

A long candlelit table was set ready for the feast, and everyone had their backs to Freddie as he slipped into the shop. It was much darker inside. He took five bottles of the orange sleeping potion and crept through to Timna's room. He didn't dare move the ladder until the feast started, so he hid behind the screen, amongst scattered papyruses, calculations and recipes – including the recipe for the solvent formula to release the magical rope!

As he kneeled to sift through the documents, his knee sank into some freshly dug soil that had been repacked into a hole. *What was going on here, then?* With a wooden spoon, he began to dig and soon hit something hard. He pulled out a leather bag, full of beads, brooches and jewellery. This must be Timna's life savings. Freddie pondered what the best punishment was for the way the sinister apothecary had treated his slaves over the years. He examined the treasure. There were several tomb medals with the symbols of long-dead pharaohs from many hundreds of years back. There was even one from Kha's reign, although the crude engraving looked nothing like his friend. *How had the apothecary come to have these ancient relics?*

A silence fell outside and Freddie stood on a table to look out of a high window. Timna began a speech to the assembled dignitaries.

"Welcome to my humble home. I can promise you good wine, great company and wonderful food." A small ripple of applause ran around the courtyard. "For those who don't know, I am Timna the apothecary, and I have lived for a thousand years." An embarrassed snigger circulated the guests. "Oh! Yes. Believe me. My medicines are magical. And I have learned how to prolong life beyond the common limits of mortality. And maybe I can do the same for you? Come and see me sometime. Meanwhile, as Osiris waits for me, he will have to be patient. I refuse to die just yet."

Awkward laughter rippled amongst the guests, but Timna continued. "Some will have heard me recite the pharaohs who have reigned in my lifetime, but for those who haven't I shall be quick, and then we can eat." The guests brightened at this. "I was born during the reign of Kheti the first…"

A rustle from beyond the screen found Ruby straining at the limit of her leash, stretching for the ladder.

"I'll do it," Freddie whispered, making Ruby jump with shock. "I've got five bottles of sleeping potion. Is that enough?" Ruby nodded and gestured to the ladder and then to the top shelf.

"I've got to go. He'll miss me," she whispered. "Give me the sleeping potion for the pudding. Meet in the outhouse. Get a dark-blue bottle." Freddie nodded and Ruby turned to go.

"Nehesy, Khyan, Apepi, Khamudi..." continued Timna's recital.

"What is he doing? It really winds me up," hissed Ruby.

"He says he's been alive a thousand years, and these are all the pharaohs he's lived under."

"That's nuts!" scoffed Ruby.

"It's good for business. Everyone will buy his potions."

"Well, how come there's not loads of thousand-year-old people wandering about?"

"...Kamose, Ahmose..."

"Good point. I'll keep listening."

Ruby crept away with the sleeping potion and Freddie silently moved the ladder. He climbed carefully in the dark and stretched for a dark blue bottle on the right-hand side of the top shelf. A noise just outside panicked him and he grabbed at the bottles, stowing one safely in Connor's backpack. Then he gathered the solvent recipe and with the other valuable papyruses he buried them in the ground where the treasure had been. They would take ages to find.

"...Seti I, Ramesses II..." still Timna droned on.

Ten times a day?' thought Freddie. He could see why it upset Ruby so much. After filling his rucksack with the apothecary's heavy bounty bag, he made his way cautiously to the outhouse.

Timna built to his usual finale, reciting the name Ramesses seven times from the third to the ninth. A slight smattering of applause greeted his conclusion, but far greater interest was caused by Connor, circulating with a platter of delicacies, as Ruby refilled people's goblets.

Then they loaded the table with food. Three types of fish, two meats, roast vegetables and sauces. Sensational aromas filled the air. Unable to hold back, the guests took their seats and filled their bowls. Timna smiled and nodded politely at the gushing compliments of his guests, but he seemed not to be hungry himself. He picked fussily at each dish, testing the flavours, but was more interested in his wine, as he smugly surveyed his influential guests.

Ruby ran to the outhouse to get another jug for Timna, and Freddie gently moved out of a shadow. Ruby jumped for the second time in half an hour.

"Stop doing that!"

"Timna's not eating. Why?"

"He was tasting Connor's cooking all afternoon."

"But what if he won't eat the yoghurt with the sleeping potion in it?" Freddie asked nervously.

"Ah! I see what you mean."

"I'll get some more and we'll put it in his wine."

Ruby returned to the table and Freddie crept back to the shop. Once his eyes adjusted to the dark, he grabbed the last two orange bottles, returned to the

225

outhouse and stirred the potions into the next two jugs.

Ruby was clearing the table and Connor was serving up the yoghurt surprise. He'd tasted a morsel to check the sleeping potion hadn't affected the flavour too much. It made it a little sour so he used Timna's entire stock of honey along with cut-up dates and figs. He circulated the gathering, ladling out huge portions. They all seemed to be lapping it up. All except the *one* person they really needed to go to sleep.

Timna tried a tiny mouthful and rolled it around his tongue, before pushing his plate away and returning to his wine. He poured himself an enormous goblet full and produced a light-blue bottle of medicine, which he plonked on the table.

Ruby checked with Freddie about the doctored wine jugs, both of which were in front of Timna. She would have to make sure they kept coming back to their hateful master.

"Take these other two jugs for the people around him, and reserve the ones with the potion in just for Timna," whispered Freddie.

"I'll try." She immediately swapped one with a sleepy man who was happy enough with his new full jug. Ruby quickly filled Timna's goblet again with the doctored wine. But now there was only one full jug left. It had to work soon or they might never escape.

Connor was accepting compliments from the sleepy

guests as he circulated the table, encouraging people to have seconds. He could see the bottle top of the solvent sticking out of Timna's pocket. He wondered about making a grab for it, but then Timna shakily stood up and threw his left arm around Connor's shoulders, using him as a support.

Ruby arrived on Timna's right to refill his goblet and he threw his other arm around her shoulder. Connor fed the drink to his grateful master and then refilled it with the doctored wine. *How much more would it take?*

Freddie could see Connor's right hand searching for the bottle of solvent and he crept low up behind Timna, who began a slurred speech.

"Now, I will show you how my med'cine works... This blue slaved hair. No! This blue haired shave... *slave* will demonstrate my magnicifent... *magnificent* talent." He grabbed the bottle and ripped the stopper out with his teeth, then pulled Ruby's face close, using the multi-coloured string.

At the third attempt, Freddie finally located the red bottle and lifted it from Timna's pocket. He tapped Connor on the back and motioned to give Timna more wine. He could see the majority of the guests' heads drooping now, and even some loud snoring emanating from those who'd been served first.

Ruby turned her head away so the medicine couldn't reach her mouth but the string was biting into her neck. Connor fed the last of the wine to his wobbling master, which he gratefully drained in one large gulp. The apothecary made one final attempt at giving Ruby the potion before suddenly dropping his arms, staring straight ahead and collapsing down onto his seat. He burped loudly, then fell forwards face down, straight into his full bowl of yoghurt surprise.

"Bingo!" said Connor.

Freddie sprinkled the magical tether with the solvent and for the first time in eight days Connor and Ruby were free. Then they gathered Ruby's long leash and wrapped Timna in it, binding him to his chair. When it came to sealing the string, their fingers wouldn't work.

"I know!" Connor whispered. He lifted Timna's hand and manipulated the apothecary's fingers to seal the restraint. Perfect! It worked first time, and Timna was securely shackled.

"Top man, Connor!" Freddie slapped his best friend on the back. They emptied the few remaining drops of solvent from the red bottle and put it upside down in front of Timna.

"I've buried the recipe for the solvent somewhere it'll take at least a week to find! So Timna will have a taste of his own medicine, literally." The friends all laughed.

"We can't hang around. They might wake up any minute," Ruby said.

Freddie gasped. "My notebook! Where is it? We won't find Kha's tomb without it!" Connor, slightly bashfully, produced a very battered and dog-eared notebook and handed it to Freddie, who inspected the food-splattered pages.

"Sorry, mate. The Kha stuff's all still there, look," he said wiping some yoghurt from the cover. Freddie thumbed quickly through the pages and smiled at Connor.

"Thanks. And it smells great, too! Let's get out of here."

They travelled as fast as they could back towards the sphinx and the vortex, and Freddie told them about Timna's loot.

"What shall we do with it all?" Ruby asked.

"I don't know yet. Something will happen, you can bet on that!" Freddie replied.

"OK, buddy. You know best," Ruby said simply.

"Listen. In the vortex, we must be joined together. So make sure as I enter Waset, that Ruby is in the tunnel and Connor is still here in Giza. Then I'll pull you both through to Waset." Freddie had used this method on arriving, with his right arm in Giza and his left arm in Waset. The time code hadn't changed as a result.

What he didn't mention was that the spirits had been fluttering about and twittering fussily. All the more reason to keep a tight hold of each other.

It was well after midnight by the time they stood by the

sphinx. No portal presented itself, so Freddie started reciting 'If—' as Connor and Ruby joined in reading from a hasty scrawl in the notebook. As the three friends reached the final verse, a shimmering purple light appeared near the base of the sphinx.

Freddie was focused and determined, Ruby felt strong and excited, and Connor, well Connor was petrified and had his eyes closed.

"Yours is the Earth and everything that's in it," the three chanted. Ruby nudged Connor to open his eyes.

"And – which is more – you'll be a Man, my son!"

It was like curtains being opened and the plasma portal instantly dissolved. Freddie entered at the far right side, looking at his friends and mouthing, "Good luck! Here we go!" He set foot into the vortex with Ruby and Connor tightly behind.

With a blustery wind rippling his hair and clothes, he inched round the divide of the two locations. Nodding first at Ruby and then Connor, whose head was just emerging through from Giza, Freddie plunged through the less fluid Waset portal. It was dying rapidly from the far side. Soon it would be firm and static, closed forever. It needed a lot of effort from Freddie to push through.

He turned to pull Ruby behind him. Just then, a flurry of cloaked spirits appeared and danced around Connor in a frenzy. A split second later, he was buffeted by the horrible darker apparition. He was knocked off his feet and only just managed to hang on to Ruby's arm. He clawed his way across the greying portal against the wind, battling to stay attached to Ruby. Her arm was the only thing he could see. His rucksack was pulled off his left shoulder, but then Connor managed to thrust his free hand into the portal. He felt two hands clasp at it as Freddie and Ruby tried with all their might to haul him through. Connor lost his grip on Ruby with his right hand and felt the rucksack easily plucked from his back by the ghostly figure. "Nooooh!"

Sensing Connor was panicking and about to let go, Freddie forced his top half back into the vortex and pulled Connor's legs with all his strength, but the ghostly apparition made a grab for Freddie, trying to claw and rip at his neck for the scarab.

Freddie grabbed at its wrist but the apparition already had its bony fingers on the precious turquoise jewel. Suddenly, a second dark figure blasted into Freddie's attacker at a thunderous speed. The demonic thief lost its grip and tumbled uncontrollably away down the vortex brandishing Connor's rucksack.

The rescuer turned, and pushed Freddie's head through the dying portal. Freddie collapsed in a heap amongst the other two in the soft grasses of the Waset glade.

"Well that was fun!" said Ruby, smiling, but looking like she was ready to collapse. "Can't wait for the return journey!"

Chapter 26

Freddie jumped up from the saturated ground. "The Inundation's started. We've got to be really quick because all this will be flooded soon, including the portal."

This news was met with looks of alarm. Connor and Ruby nodded and they all squelched through the cold night in damp clothes to higher ground, being careful to make no noise.

"We'll go straight to the Valley of the Kings," Freddie whispered. "We've only got one torch left. Save it for the tomb."

"No problem." Ruby nodded excitedly.

Connor was moaning about stones in his sandals, so the trio paused to give him a second to clear the debris away. They were about to set off again when they saw flaming torches approaching along the path.

"Quick, down here!" Ruby whispered, gesturing to a handy water channel. They deftly slipped in, shoulder deep, and watched a group of twenty or so angry-looking men jog past. Freddie recognised them right away.

"What was that all about?" asked Connor.

"That's the right-hand gang. They've escaped. I heard them say soldiers were following them and they're arguing about where to go next."

"We've got to be careful," said Ruby.

"Yes," Freddie agreed. "Let's use this channel. The road's too dangerous."

Moving through the water slowed their progress, but it was worth it as they avoided two squads of soldiers and then a large group of women and children who were escaping to join their menfolk. Freddie hoped they would make it safely past the brutal troops.

"There must have been a riot. They haven't been fed properly for ages. I'm not surprised there's been a rebellion."

As they hid, another group of workers passed by, shadows against the starry sky. Freddie overheard them say that when the left-hand gang finished the night shift, they were bound to mutiny as well. He wondered if he should relay this to Connor and Ruby. There couldn't be a more dangerous and unpredictable time to be heading for Kha's tomb.

To avoid the worker's path, Freddie took Connor

and Ruby the long way round via the valley entrance. They hid high on the slope above Ramesses IX's tomb so they could watch the left-hand gang leave.

As the sun came up, Freddie saw the hateful Bek stride from the tomb entrance. A dozen soldiers running down the worker's path towards him immediately grabbed his attention. They exchanged news and as the left-hand gang wearily emerged from their night's work, they were immediately shackled by the soldiers to prevent any attempt at escape. Pawah, the tall leader, protested loudly, but Bek struck him with a vicious blow and the group trudged miserably away.

Freddie waited until the gang had crested the ridge and scanned the hillside around, before skittering down the scree slope towards the safety of the three workers' huts. Connor and Ruby were not far behind him and they caught their breath squatting against the stone wall of the end shack.

Connor watched Freddie consult his notes, making sure the coast was clear before he ventured out on to the valley floor. He paced about as if measuring his position. Ruby and Connor exchanged concerned looks as he zigzagged about like a tormented spider. This didn't look good. Freddie looked up to the distinctive summit of Ta Dehent, before adjusting his position five metres or so to his right. He scuffed a mark in the dust, then paced 25 metres straight ahead, but came up against the wall of the next hut. He turned to the other two. "I'm three metres short. The entrance must be under here."

They burst through the door of the stonemason's shelter. Freddie paced three metres from the wall and ended up standing on top of the raised stone slab that was the mason's work surface. The three shared a defeated look. "How are we going to shift *that*?" Ruby sighed.

"The crane thingy. That might lift it!" Connor pointed to the shadoof. It was certainly sturdy, but the slab was at least four feet square and a foot thick.

"Worth a try," Freddie said. They knotted some thick hemp rope over the crane's arm and secured it tightly with three turns, then tied it round the exposed corners of the block. All three ran to the counterweight of the shadoof and put all their efforts into pulling it down. The rope went taut and made worrying creaking noises. Then, just as Connor thought it was hopeless, the stone shifted a fraction. They rested for thirty seconds, gathered their strength and tried again. This time the stone moved slightly and they turned the shadoof to the right at the same time. Again they rested, but when they tried a third time, the stone swung clear of a gaping hole. Connor felt like whooping out loud.

Ruby pointed at him. "You star," she said.

"Wow!" said Connor, feeling his cheeks go red in

the semi-dark.

Freddie touched the scarab at his neck. He knew he was doing all he possibly could to keep a promise.

With Connor's rucksack stolen, and the blue elixir and his torch along with it, Ruby shone their one remaining beam down the long pipe tunnel as two centuries of stale air wafted up at them from the dark.

"You go first, Freddie, he's your friend," Ruby suggested. Freddie nodded and positioned himself over the hole. He lowered himself gently down, calling back, "There's little ridges to put your feet on so you don't slip." And with that, the light and Freddie disappeared from view. Ruby grabbed at the rucksack and got the camera out.

Freddie shone the torch up. "I'm down. It's OK. Who's next?" Ruby began her descent. In half the time, her call came back to Connor. He took a deep breath and positioned himself to descend, but he was just too big for the narrow opening. He wasn't just a bit too big, he was *far* too big for it. As hard as he tried, he couldn't even get his hips and tummy into the gap. His heart sank and he swallowed hard.

"C'mon, mate, you can do it," said Freddie. But it was hopeless.

"I can't, I can't get my... Ugh! I'm stuck." Connor felt like a human champagne cork. He floundered around and tried to pull himself back out, eventually grabbing and dislodging the rope from the stone slab. With enormous effort he hauled himself clear and lay on the floor of the hut, exhausted and embarrassed. For him, the glories of King Tutankhamun's tomb would remain photos in library books.

"You carry on. I'll keep guard up here. Say hello to Kha from me please, Freddie," he called to his friends, silently cursing himself for missing out.

"Sorry, mate," Freddie called up. "We won't be long. Keep watch." Freddie dropped to the floor and located the two levers in the torch's beam. He knew time was short and went straight to the lever on the right that would open the treasury wall. From there they would get through the tiny low opening to the burial chamber.

"Here goes!" He pulled at the lever, but only when Ruby grasped hold of it to help did the stones creak slowly round. Freddie pushed his arms through with the torch, then his head.

Ruby held her breath as he disappeared. "Oh! Wow! Ruby, look at this!" She followed excitedly behind him, and the two friends stood spellbound in the most famous treasury in the whole of history.

Freddie slowly shone the torch around the small chamber, which was packed with hundreds of treasures. Their eyes were greeted by a wonderful sight. On their left, looking through the low door to the burial chamber was the jackal-headed god Anubis, swathed in a linen cloth on its sled. On their right was the gloriously decorated gold canopic shrine, which was almost as tall as the ceiling. The head of the Hathor cow was in front of them and dozens of model sailing boats with intricate masts and rigging were placed on top of funerary chests. Several caskets were set in a neat line, beyond Anubis, with their lids askew. It was obvious that robbers had been here and targeted them, as they had contained jewels that could easily be carried away.

"I'm so glad I didn't put the scarab here before the robbers came," Freddie whispered to Ruby who had been staring open-mouthed at everything. She took photos in all directions as they slowly picked their way past the priceless objects and stood nervously by the low gap to the burial chamber.

Freddie shone the torch through and a golden light immediately bounced back at them. The huge casings of the sarcophagus reflected the torch's beam and dazzled them, sending shards of reflected light about the room. It was breathtakingly beautiful. The low base that Freddie had hidden behind when he was listening to Ay and Userhat now contained Kha's body, which lay deep inside this huge golden tomb. It was obvious that the robbers had searched for the scarab, as two of the ornate outer casings had been forced open.

While Ruby held the torch, Freddie carefully removed the turquoise beetle from the string around his neck. He gently teased the heavy doors of the outer cabinet further open, ceremoniously kissed the scarab and placed it on a tiny ledge on the door of the second casement. It was the obvious place for it to go, as a perfect inlaid carving of the beetle adorned the panel behind it.

Freddie's fingers lingered on the tiny object. He closed his eyes and wished his friend a safe passage to the next world. Now that Kha's guardian was finally with him, Freddie's promise was fulfilled and his work was done.

The moment was only broken by a searing flash as Ruby captured the image on the disposable camera. It felt wrong as soon as the camera clicked. She winced as the harsh, white light receded.

"Sorry," she whispered. "Sorry, Freddie. Sorry, Kha."

Freddie nodded. "It's OK, I've kept my promise to him and Ankha. They won't mind." Freddie didn't want Ruby to feel bad.

He was reluctant to leave the last resting place of his friend, and sat quietly by the golden tomb, looking around in wonder. It was one thing to see pictures in books but it was quite another to witness them up close and for real.

Ruby explored the tight space. There was less than a metre between the outer panels of the sarcophagus and the burial chamber walls. She tiptoed between the eleven wooden oars laid out on the floor. The decorated yellow walls with their beautifully crafted paintings seemed to welcome Ruby's torchlight.

"Look at this," whispered Ruby. Freddie joined her and they stared in wonder at the west wall that depicted the Solar Barque following five gods across the sky. Underneath sat twelve squat baboons, who each represented an hour of the night, through which the sun and the king must travel before achieving rebirth at dawn. Now Kha had his guardian scarab, his journey could begin.

The torch beam flickered. "We'd better think about going," Freddie said. "I'd like to stay for hours but—"

"It's OK. We'll remember it forever and I've taken loads of photos," Ruby replied.

After allowing Freddie a final quiet moment alone in the burial chamber, the two carefully retraced their steps through the treasury, making sure nothing was disturbed. It took both of them to revolve the stones, with the lever only slightly less stiff than before.

Ruby couldn't resist one last excursion. After all, this was the chance of a lifetime.

"Can we just have a peek in the antechamber before we go? We won't be long. Just a quick look, I promise. It's silly to come all this way and not see it."

"The torch is running low."

"Just a little look," Ruby begged. "I'll take some pics and then we'll get going."

Freddie nodded. "All right, but we can't stay long. Connor! Connor?"

"Yeah?" came the muffled reply, "I've found some bread and stuff, I've saved you some."

"Great. We're just going to look in the antechamber and then we'll be out. Is it all OK up there?"

"Yeah. Fine. I do a search every five minutes. Nothing going on up here."

"Wait for our call, mate, OK?" said Freddie.

"OK."

Freddie pulled the left lever. It lifted easily and the stones moved swiftly round. They found themselves next to two statues of life-sized, gold-shendyt-clad, black-faced guards either side of the blocked entrance to the burial chamber.

As Freddie moved the torch beam round to the left, his breath was taken away. Three familiar day couches, with wonderfully carved animal post heads, stood against the far wall, crammed with treasures and relics. It felt like Kha and Ankha would spring back to life any second.

He continued to shine the beam left, and a jumble of chariot wheels littered the end of the chamber, but it was easy to pick out the passenger cage of the golden chariot as it perched on top of everything else. It pierced a dazzling reflection back, even in the weakening beam of the torch. Suddenly, saving Kha's life at the massacre of the bulls seemed a very long time ago to Freddie.

This room was a mess compared to the treasury. Things had very obviously been disturbed. Freddie felt like he wanted to tidy up, as if it wasn't in a fit state to celebrate his friend's life.

As the torch flickered again, a rising sense of panic in the pair led them to cut short their tour. With a final panorama shot of the room, they turned to leave.

But something had changed! Freddie's senses screamed a red alert. He stared in horror at the place they had entered through, and then at Ruby.

There was no gap!

Instead, fine sand poured through where the two stones had turned. Ruby looked aghast, her blue eyes wide with fear.

"Where's that come from?"

The sand flowed like water into the room. Freddie had to think quickly. He shouted to Ruby.

"You go. I'll push you from this side. Then I'll do the same and you pull me through. Make sure Connor's on standby. Take the torch! Deep breath. Go, Go, Go!"

Ruby didn't waste a second. She thrust her body through the fine sand and with Freddie pushing at her feet, she gradually disappeared from the antechamber. Now Freddie was completely in the dark. He dropped to the floor on his front, took a huge deep breath and pushed his body, fighting against the great weight of sand that was filling the gap behind the secret entrance.

He battled away, almost swimming with his arms to create space that he could then get his body into. His right leg scraped painfully against the lever mechanism and the leather straps of his sandal caught over the handle. He was nearly at the end of his breath, floundering around with his arms to try and stand on the pipe tunnel side of the wall. Suddenly he felt Ruby's feet and then her hand plunged down, grabbing his right shoulder, then, a second later taking a firm hold under his arm. She began to drag him upright, but his sandal was still stuck on the lever. He pulled his foot up and pushed it down again, closing the stone entrance to the antechamber. No sand could get through there now, but it meant it was filling the gap their side of the wall even faster.

The sandal straps tore away and with Ruby's help Freddie was at last free to stand. He broke the surface and gasped for air, amazed that the sand was already chest-high and rising. It was pouring in from gaps under the tiny footholds in the pipe tunnel. This must be the surprise the hateful Userhat had meant when he was talking to Ay. It was a trap and they were being buried alive. Freddie couldn't let Userhat win!

Ruby was shorter than Freddie, and already had her face turned upwards to stop the grains getting in her mouth. She shouted up desperately. "Help! Help us, Connor! Throw a rope down, quickly."

"What's going on?" came the bewildered reply as

he peered into the pitch-black tunnel. The torch had been lost in the panic.

"Quickly, Connor, it's filling up... it's... Aah! We're going to drown! Help us!" Freddie grabbed Ruby round the waist and lifted her up so she could breathe, but still the sand came. Ruby tried to brush it aside but it was so fine that it levelled out like a pond.

"CONNOR!"

From above them came a shout. "Here's the rope!" A second or two later the thick hemp that had lifted the vast stone snaked its way down towards them. But it fell just short of Ruby's outstretched arm and Freddie had to lift with all his might to push her up until she could grab it. Ruby wound it around her wrist and tried to pull Freddie with her as Connor rushed to the counterweight end of the shadoof and heaved down with all his might. Ruby emerged from the sand holding Freddie's arm, trying with all her strength to lift him with her, but the weight of both of them was too much for Connor.

"You go, Ruby. Then drop the rope back down for me. Go, now! Pull, Connor. Pull!"

Ruby began rising up the pipe and after Connor had wedged the shadoof's arm, he ran round and hauled her to the surface, every muscle exploding with effort.

All the while the sand was rising about Freddie. He tried to raise himself, but it was hopeless. It was up to his ears and all he could hear was muffled shouts from above. He was trying not to panic and prepare for a huge final breath for when the sand would cover his head.

At the top, Ruby hauled herself up and out of the entrance. She flung the rope back down the pipe for Freddie while Connor released the counterweight end and raised it as high as it would go.

Ruby yelled down to Freddie, "The rope's coming. Grab it, Freddie!"

In the dark abyss below, Freddie's nose was turned upwards with his arms flailing blindly to find the end of the rope as it danced wildly above him. His fingertips brushed it, but he just couldn't quite reach it. Ruby jumped up and undid one turn of the rope on the shadoof. But would that be enough? She felt a sickness in her stomach and the purest terror took hold. She looked at Connor's stricken features as he desperately waited for the signal to lift.

Freddie's head was now under the sand and his hand floundered in the air, searching desperately.

There! There it was! His fingers tightened on the rope's frayed end and he felt for a better grip. His other hand shot up to grab above that. With the combination of the last trace of his strength, and Connor, heaving down on the counterweight end, Ruby saw the battered and panting figure of Freddie Malone emerge slowly from the cascading sand!

While Connor wedged the counterweight again,

Ruby stood astride the pipe's mouth, hauling the rope up single-handedly.

"Pull me up. Quick! Pull me up!" Freddie gasped as the deluge of fine sand fell away from him.

Connor and Ruby had saved Freddie's life.

They had cheated death, and they had cheated Ay and Userhat. What's more, Freddie had done his duty and carried out his promise.

As all three lay in a panting and exhausted heap on the floor, they smiled the broadest grins possible.

Freddie turned on his side and spitting out sand said, "Well that all went smoothly! Ruby could you go back down and get my other sandal, please?"

Chapter 27

It took ages to reattach the rope and move the huge slab back into place. The effort nearly finished them off. But once Connor had shared out the provisions and water he'd found in the next hut, they all began to feel vaguely human once again.

Suddenly, Ruby gasped. "The camera! I can't find it. It must be in the sand. Oh no! All those photos. Now we can't show anyone."

"We couldn't anyway," said Freddie, quietly.

"The adventures are just between us," Connor pointed out. "No one else can *ever* know." Ruby nodded sadly.

"I could do with some of that blue medicine that was in Connor's rucksack," said Freddie.

"Are you sure you got the dark-blue one?" asked Ruby.

"I think so, but it was a bit of a stretch and I panicked a bit."

"Well, someone's going to either feel a million dollars or spend a week throwing up!" she said smiling.

They rested and gathered their strength before making sure nothing gave away the tunnel or their presence there.

Checking all was clear, the three friends set off for the portal as the light began to fade. The fresh air was a welcome change. Sand had got into every tiny crease of their skin. Freddie was constantly wiping and shaking the remnants away, whilst teaching Ruby – and reminding Connor – of the poem 'If—', their homeward mantra.

Keeping to the safety of the irrigation ditches, and guided by a full moon, they saw no signs of anyone until they got nearer the Nile.

They shrunk into the bank as a group of soldiers led by Bek jogged past them. All Freddie heard Bek say was, "We can cut them off at the jetty. They'll be trying to cross the river." Freddie knew this was dangerous news, as the jetty and the portal were only a few hundred metres apart.

As they made for the silhouette of the rocky outcrop in the bright moonlight, they could see the extent of the flooding. Even since their arrival last night, the water had risen considerably. It was above waist height as they got to the dead palm tree with its top leaning against the steep stone. They climbed out of the water so Freddie could work out the direction of their escape route. Suddenly, a powerful hand clasped Ruby's shoulder and pulled her away.

"Freddie! Con—" she screamed, but another large hand clamped her mouth shut.

"Who have we here?" echoed Bek's voice, as he handed Ruby to the soldiers, before easily catching Connor and handing him over too. Freddie watched in horror at this new disaster.

"Run, Freddie!" shouted Ruby, struggling with her captors.

Freddie hooked his rucksack safely out of sight of Bek and scampered crab-like up the rocky slope in just one sandal.

"You won't escape me, scribe," Bek thundered. "You started all this! Because of you, the others got big ideas. They thought they could do the same. Well no one escapes my justice. Come here and take your punishment."

However quickly Freddie climbed, the stronger soldiers were gaining on him rapidly. But as he neared the top of the outcrop, he suddenly saw twenty or thirty human shapes, outlined across the crest of the rock, holding cudgels and swords. Freddie was trapped.

Then one of the dark shapes shouted his name. "Intef, Intef, it's us, the men of the left-hand! Get behind us." Pawar turned to his comrades. "Get the soldiers, boys, but leave Bek to me. I owe him a little something."

Attacking from above, Freddie's friends easily overpowered the enemy and scattered them into the water, now chest-high. Most of the soldiers dived off the rock rather than face a fight, and the guards holding Connor and Ruby abandoned them when they saw the fight was lost.

Ruby grabbed the rucksack before it floated away, and joined Freddie and his friends halfway up the rock. A cheer went up as the hero scribe 'Intef' was enveloped into the ranks of his former comrades. After all, he'd kept salt in the wicks and stopped the torches smoking. Connor staggered to his feet and stood alongside his friend overwhelmed by another close shave.

"Thank you for saving us," Freddie said. "These are my friends from Albanicus. But how did you escape? We saw the soldiers shackle you this morning."

Pawar laughed and boomed in his deep voice, "We are the left-hand gang, and neither flint nor chains get in our way." His men joined in the loud cheer that followed.

Freddie then said, "We need you to do one more thing for us. In return, I have something special for you." He spoke the Egyptian words slowly, so there would be no misunderstandings. Then he opened the rucksack, took out the bag of Timna's treasure and handed it to Pawar along with the remaining jewels from Ankha's necklace. "Please split this between yourselves and start new lives." The men were amazed and bombarded Freddie with questions, but he simply smiled and said, "They're a gift from a very old friend – A *very, very* old friend." Ruby and Connor smiled knowingly. Then Freddie locked forearms with each man in friendly salute and accepted their thanks.

"What is it you want us to do, Intef?" said the astonished Pawar.

"It sounds mad, but when we're at the top of that dead palm tree, I want you to push it away into the water. I hope the bottom of the tree will wedge in that cleft of rock behind it. The top should fall over there." Freddie pointed to a place well upstream of where the portal was likely to appear under water. If his calculations were correct about where the palm would fall, they would then have to jump into the water and be swept in the current towards the portal. Then dive down to find its entrance. In his mind he could see his Uncle Patrick scratching his head with doubt. It was a crazy gamble he knew, but it was the only plan they had.

"When we're safely at the top, wait for my signal, Pawar. Then push." He pointed again in the direction they had to aim for and directed Connor and Ruby to climb the rock and transfer to the treetop. After the madness of the last few hours, Connor was ready to give this latest plan his best shot. Ruby, too, who beamed an excited smile at this new challenge. She watched as two of the men, realising the difficulty Connor was having, helped the heavy, exhausted boy up to a safe position, lodging him in the crook of the two-headed tree. Ruby and Freddie scampered higher, either side of him, one on each head.

Freddie waited for the men to get out of the way and then, pointing in front of him he shouted, "NOW! Hold on, guys. Let's get out of here." The three friends began to recite 'If—'.

It took a massive effort for the men to push the huge, dead tree away from the rock, but if anyone could do it, the left-hand gang could. Gradually it passed the point of no return and, as they started the third verse, the tree slowly tilted downwards and then built up speed as it crashed down into the deep water below. They just about held on and survived the plunge, with their hearts largely in their mouths.

The tree's base was wedged solidly in the cleft as Freddie had hoped. With the current racing across them, they had to get to the end of 'If—' and see where the portal appeared. Freddie hoped it would light up, like an underwater airport runway.

Great chunks of debris buffeted the huge tree trunk and it refused to move, but it shuddered with the force of the collisions and the ferocious current.

All of a sudden, an angry shout split the night air.

"Aarrghh! I'll get you, scribe!" From the shadows, Freddie saw Bek scramble onto the palm's trunk. After finding his balance, he began advancing up the floating tree towards them.

The left-hand gang began pelting him with rocks. Four or five hit him painfully and stalled his progress. Freddie held his breath as the brute struggled murderously on towards them. He dropped to his knees and crawled along, shouting revenge and promising the scribe a terrible end.

Bek was closing on them fast and Connor was going to be first in the firing line, so he began inching further up Freddie's branch, which didn't like the extra weight at all. Now they were all clustered at the two tops of the split tree.

A huge dark shape buffeted the trunk midway between them and Bek, driven against the tree by the force of the current. It was smooth and about the size of a car. Suddenly a head emerged from its far end and a huge set of jaws belonging to one of the infamous Nile hippopotamuses opened and shut. The three instantly stopped reciting.

They all stared in awe at the huge beast. *What else could Egypt throw at them?* Freddie thought, before pulling himself together and carrying on with his mantra. They had to get to the end, fast.

The rocks were still flying at Bek, who had gone silent since seeing the hippo. One well-aimed stone struck him on the shoulder and another, rather aptly, thrown by Pawar, hit Bec on his left hand, dislodging it from the tree trunk. He recoiled in pain, lost his balance and screamed in terror as he toppled into the water, quickly followed by the diving hippo.

Nothing was seen of either of them again. But the moment of respite was quickly replaced by a new panic. The hippo's attacking dive at Bek had severed the palm where the two tops joined the main trunk, so they were now adrift and began to swing left in the current.

"Be ready to jump," Freddie shouted. He heard two firm replies of "OK!"

As they neared the final lines of 'If—', a shimmering purple light appeared deep in the water to their left. Freddie felt a surge of relief at the sight of their unmistakable gateway home.

The current toyed with the huge tree in the midst of the dark flood and the three friends swayed nervously as they spoke the final lines.

"Yours is the Earth and everything that's in it,

And – which is more – you'll be a Man, my son!"

All three got ready to jump. Connor and Ruby waited to follow Freddie's lead. They dived into the frothing mass at least 50 metres before the portal and plunged deep under water. The surge carried them onwards. Freddie, then Ruby, timed it perfectly and were swallowed gratefully into the vortex. Connor could see his two friends had nailed this final challenge and knew instantly that his buoyancy would mean his escape was going to be slightly more problematical. He hit the top of the portal, which was two metres below the surface. Connor made a desperate grab but the pressure of the water hampered his movement. He couldn't hang on and was seconds from being carried away, but then he felt four hands take a sure hold of him. Finally, a hooded figure leaned through the portal and pulled Connor firmly inside. As quickly as the guardian spirit had appeared, it vanished.

The three friends hurtled at speed, bouncing off the walls along the vortex. This time, Connor enjoyed every second of the ride. As they crashed into each other at the dead end of the tunnel, they shared a look of wonder.

Then Freddie said, "Shall I do the honours?" He plunged the multi-tool into the vortex wall and the resulting gap allowed Freddie, then Ruby, and finally Connor to flop through like breathless fish onto Freddie's bedroom floor.

The first thing they saw was the ice sculpture of Jasper and Kelvin still leaning against the wardrobe. The map wobbled, as if shaking off a rain shower and in a few seconds reformed perfectly, with the beautiful sight of Tutankhamun's famous mask now nestling below the pyramids on the distinctive bend in the Nile. Then the whole map solidified with one final ripple of satisfaction after Neptune had blown a jet of warm air in Jasper and Kelvin's direction.

It was now just after 4:30 pm.

"We've only been gone two hours!" gasped Connor.

"Great! I said to my mum I'd be home by five!" Ruby smiled.

They were amazed. Absolutely amazed and exhausted. They stared at the two gatecrashers, who were gradually thawing.

"Let's use my brothers' go-cart and take them to the bench by the postbox. We can leave them there with Hallowe'en masks on or something," said Ruby, with a glint in her eye. All three fist-bumped. Ruby rushed home, changed and grabbed the go-cart.

A very groggy Jasper was untied and loaded onto the cart and wheeled down Normandy Avenue in the gathering dusk. Connor, now dressed in one of Mr M's tracksuits, was left on guard. He wrote a card about collecting for Hallowe'en and placed it next to the bully. Freddie and Ruby soon returned with Kelvin and once both were loosely tied together, they had babyish Hallowe'en masks put over their faces. Finally, as Kelvin started to show signs of waking up, the three scampered back up the road.

Mr and Mrs M pulled up in their car, returning from visiting Finnegan in hospital, and the trio arranged to meet in the park at ten the next day. All of a sudden, Connor was left standing alone on the pavement feeling very lonely and flummoxed. He lingered in case either of the others popped back out with a meal invitation, but none came.

He wanted to stop at the fish and chip shop on the way home, but he looked down at his waistline and remembered how he'd felt back at Kha's tomb, when he couldn't fit down the pipe. He was torn.

He decided to go straight home, open all the cupboards, and create a feast using anything that came to hand. Even if there were no fresh ingredients, he would pretend that whatever was there were delicious jewels from an exotic market somewhere, and he had expectant guests to cook for.

Epilogue

Freddie dreamed he was lying on a beach, slowly sinking into sand. He awoke in a panic to find his bedclothes flung over the floor where he'd wrestled them off.

Ruby researched for two hours and looked up every website and photo of Kha's tomb she could find. Everything was as they'd left it. There was no mention of a pipe tunnel, because of course it had never been found.

After wrestling with a can of chickpeas, an onion, and some out-of-date Madras curry paste, Connor gave in and resorted to the frozen pizza that was luring him from the across the kitchen. He consoled himself that it was slightly healthier than usual with the sweet potato fries he heaped on the side. As he fell asleep he had one final thought. He had done all right, all things considered!

In the morning, Freddie, having been so decisive and clear of thought in Egypt, couldn't make up his mind which socks to put on and had trouble leaving the house, going back twice for things he'd forgotten.

Ruby, having single-handedly lifted Freddie out of the sand to safety, couldn't even open the marmalade jar at breakfast and had to have help to carry the rubbish out to the dustbin.

And Connor, after creating several glorious meals and even a feast for a dozen people, burned his toast and then cut his finger buttering it!

It was the last day of half-term and it was hard to contemplate school tomorrow. The three sat in a daze, occasionally saying things like, "I wonder what happened to Menna and his cart?" or "Do you think Bek survived the hippo attack?" or "What would we have done with all that jewellery?" Each question was followed by a long silence as they were lost in their own thoughts, still in an exotic land a long way away, and many years ago.

"My mum says I've got to dye my hair back to normal tonight, for school," Ruby uttered, resentfully. "Don't worry though, I usually colour it red over Christmas!"

"NO!" said Connor rather too loudly, "I mean,

please don't, I like it blue."

"So do I, you look great," agreed Freddie.

"Yeah, you look beau— err, you look great—"

Interrupting Connor in the nick of time, Trevor the park-keeper drove past in his new electric cart. "My chariot, I call it." He laughed, but was a little taken aback at how funny the three friends found his joke.

"Who's this, then?" Trevor nodded.

"Our new friend, Ruby," Freddie told him, proudly.

"Yeah! Ruby, our new *best* friend," added Connor, in case Trevor was in any doubt.

"All right, buddy?" she offered, breezily. "Nice wheels!"

"Thanks. Good to meet you, Ruby. Go careful on these boys. Look after them, because they have a hard time looking after themselves." With that he chortled off in his silent chariot back to his hut and his tea break.

"It's all in that big museum in Cairo, all Kha's stuff. Like his chariot and, well, *everything*. We should go and see it one day," Ruby suggested. She looked across at the two boys with her pretty sapphire-blue eyes. "I like your *'stuff'*. Never thought it would be this amazing," she said.

"I wonder where we'll go next," mused Connor dreamily.

"Wow! Give us a chance," laughed Freddie. He couldn't believe the three of them were back in one piece. It had been a close call, more than once. The two people either side of him had been epic. Strong in mind and body. He was only alive because of them. They were completely awesome.

"But I've got to say it's so much better with you guys. It was really hard doing it all alone. We really worked well together. Thank you. You're both incredible." Connor beamed and Ruby nodded.

"I can't wait," she said, grinning.

Whilst finishing their ice creams they saw an ambulance rush past the park with its sirens blaring. "That reminds me, Finnegan's still in hospital. He's got some terrible stomach thing. He's really ill and he's gone a bit odd. He tried to discharge himself yesterday afternoon and disappeared from his ward for a couple of hours. Dad found him lying on a bench in the hospital garden."

"What?"

"Yeah, my mum and dad had just taken Kathleen out for a sandwich and Finnegan disappeared. They found him clutching his belly and screaming in pain."

Connor didn't want anyone to suffer pain, but if anyone had to, especially after his behaviour in the library, somehow Finnegan deserved it.

"Uncle Patrick had to babysit for me last night

coz my parents were sorting Kathleen out. Look what he bought me from a charity shop." Freddie opened his rucksack and pulled out a battered jigsaw box. Ruby and Connor gasped and smiled with delight as they saw the beautiful picture on the front. There was the glorious sight of the pyramids at sunset, set back from the sphinx in the foreground.

"What do you make of that?" asked Freddie, lost in the mystery of it all. The three friends stared at the box for ages, looking at the view they knew so well.

"It must be a coincidence, that's all," said Ruby eventually.

Connor pulled a face. "That's spooky."

"What about Jasper and Kelvin?" said Freddie, suddenly. Connor laughed. "I walked past them again on my way home. Kelvin was shaking Jasper, who was making funny little, mouse-like noises. I hid behind a van and then Jasper woke up and said, 'What's going on? What happened?' and Kelvin said, 'I don't know... I can't remember. Someone must have ambushed us.'" Connor laughed again. "I watched them go and then I grabbed the masks and rope. And guess what? They'd collected well over three pounds from people. So the next ice cream is on Jasper and Kelvin."

"I hope they don't remember what happened.

We'll have to come up with a plan in case they do," said Freddie.

"Yeah we'll need a plan all right," Ruby replied with a little chuckle.

"We'll think of something! We always do. But maybe we should have another ice cream first, eh?" said Connor, rattling the coins and smiling.

Author's Notes:
The Facts Behind the Story

Thank you for reading Freddie Malone's second adventure. There are more to come! Some of you may be interested to know what's true and what's not in the pages you've just read. Let's start with the boy king himself.

Every book gives a different age for **Tutankhamun's** accession to the throne and his death. The dates I have used for his reign are 1333–1323 BC (remember we're going backwards towards zero). I have said this happened between the ages of 9 and 19. but it might have been 8 and 18, or 8 and 19. Most scholars think it is unlikely he reached his 20th birthday.

He was the penultimate ruler of the 18th dynasty in a period called the 'New Kingdom'; Ay was the last.

The latest research indicates Kha had a condition known as temporal lobe epilepsy, which would have caused seizures and blackouts. He certainly had a cleft palate and a club left foot, which would have dramatically affected his movement and body shape. He was undoubtedly weak in body, and at times in mind. This was caused by the policy of inter-marrying within Egyptian royalty, which meant their offspring were more susceptible to inherited diseases.

For many years people thought a mark at the base of Kha's skull was caused by a blow during an attempted assassination. The latest research disputes this. Septicaemia from a badly broken leg may have actually ended his life.

Most scholars agree that **Ankhesenamun** did marry Ay after Tutankhamun's death, but much against her will. She hated Ay and pleaded by letter to the neighbouring Hittite king, begging him to send one of his sons for her to marry. Prince Zannanza set off to do just that, but he was murdered on his way to Egypt.

Ay – old enough to be Ankha's grandfather – ruled for six years, leaving the 18th dynasty in a less than stable state. The military took over in the guise of Horemheb as pharaoh, as the 19th dynasty got underway.

Information about Ankha's story fades after her marriage to Ay, almost as if she disappeared. The search for her burial place continues. If it is ever discovered, we will find out so much more.

It is recorded that Tutankhamun had a dog called

Dedu. The modern-day breed of pharaoh hounds are of the same blood line as the Tesem hunting dogs that were popular in ancient Egypt. It strikes me that the carved image of Anubis, found in the treasury in Kha's tomb, is positioned as close to the foot of his sarcophagus as possible, just as a loyal dog waits at the feet of its master. Was it placed there on Ankha's instructions? Who knows?

Tutankhamun's tomb is accurately described except for my additions of the pipe tunnel and two turning stone block entrances.

Over 5,000 separate treasures and artefacts were found by Howard Carter and Lord Carnarvon on or after the 26th November 1922. The following year the burial chamber was officially opened.

It was immediately obvious someone had been there before them, as there were signs of disturbance, pilfering and crude attempts to cover the robbery, though it seems only small, highly valuable objects were stolen. Experts agree this happened in the first few years after Tutankhamun was buried – so almost definitely by someone with inside knowledge about where to look and what to steal. Most likely the culprit was directly involved in the building or stocking of the tomb.

Tomb 62 was originally built for Ay and was swapped

The Great Pyramid and the Great Sphinx at Giza

to house Tutankhamun in some haste. As Kha had died much earlier than expected, the grander, royal tomb complex was not yet ready for him. As was the custom, his body had to be interred exactly 70 days after death and so a substitute tomb had to be found. The paintwork in Kha's burial chamber has bacterial and fungal growth on some walls. Some say this is because the tomb was sealed while the paint was still drying. Kha's original tomb was either KV23 or KV25 in the West Valley.

I have invented Kha's **scarab** and its intended position on his sarcophagus. However, much of the symbolism seen on jewellery and wall paintings features the beetle. It was a symbol of perseverance, mimicking the sun's journey through the night, being rolled by the god Khepri. His actions were echoed in real life by the beetle pushing its ball of dung.

The first burial in the **Valley of the Kings** was Thutmose I (1492 BC). Tutankhamun was the seventh pharaoh to be interred there. Eighty or more tombs and pits have been discovered so far. Sadly, many have already been robbed of their treasures.

Akhet, the annual flood did happen. The water level

at Waset rose by an estimated 35 feet and helped to create fertile land around the river Nile. This ceased to happen when the Aswan low dam was built in 1902, followed by the Aswan high dam, constructed between 1960 and 1970.

All place names in the book are real. **Thebes** is the modern name for what was **Waset,** at the time the largest and most important city in the world. **Cairo** emerged from **Memphis.**

The **Karnak Temple Complex** is the largest religious structure ever built.

I have tried to use **names** common in the 18th Dynasty. **Maya** the grand architect was indeed 'Overseer of works in the place of eternity'. **Horemheb**'s assistant, **Minnakht,** was a close relative of **Ay,** and was planted as a spy close to Horemheb so he could report back to Ay on his rival's intentions.

The **workers of Pa Demi** were separated into left-hand and right-hand gangs that worked in alternating shifts. Had they worked at the same time in the close confines of the underground chambers, their swinging tools would have knocked each other out!

Ram-headed sphinxes at Karnak

The **strikes and riots** were a common feature around the time that Ramesses IX tomb was under construction. It is thought that in previous centuries the workers were well looked after and prized as specialists, but that had all changed 200 years on from Tutankhamun.

Bull hunts were all too common as both training exercises for charioteers, and sport.

Language. Even if Freddie had written 100 pages of modern Egyptian vocabulary in his notebook for his first trip there, no one would have understood him. At the separate times of 1328 and 1125 BC that I feature in this book, the language used would have been the 'Late Egyptian Language'. An Afroasiatic language.

Bartering. Gems, beads and jewellery of all types were traded for staple necessities. Goods were swapped, fish for bread and corn for fruit and so on. Everything had a value and could be traded – even people! It would be another 500 years before coins became commonly used.

It has been a pleasure to immerse myself in all things Egyptian whilst writing this Freddie Malone adventure. I hope I've inspired you to do the same.

Thanks

Thank you to my inspirational agent Penny Luithlen, and to Anna, Fiona and the team at Award Publications.

To the thousands of students who listened with patience and enthusiasm to my talks about Nepal and Everest for *The Treasure at the Top of the World*.

Thank you also for the wonderful reaction from *you*, the readers. It proved a constant motivator as 'Jewel' took shape. Your feedback is absolutely vital and eagerly anticipated.

To all who voted, and helped 'Treasure' win the People's Book Prize 2019. Your support is incredible.

Thank you, Mick and Sandra Newman, Barnaby Eaton-Jones and Bernadette Brady for your flag waving and encouragement.

I am very grateful to my brothers Keith and Richard. I feel very lucky to be a Mantle.

Finally, thank you to my wonderful parents, Pat and Harold, who sacrificed so much to see me educated, equipped and enthused. And to my fantastic son Harry and glorious wife Carla, for their endless encouragement, strength, inspiration and love.